2005

THE BETROTHAL

Other books by Joan Vincent:

The Promise Rose

THE BETROTHAL

•

Joan Vincent

AVALON BOOKS
NEW YORK

PRINTED IN THE UNITED STATES OF AMERICA
ON ACID-FREE PAPER
BY HADDON CRAFTSMEN, BLOOMSBURG, PENNSYLVANIA

Thanks to each and every one of you
for your encouragement and prayers:
Family and Friends
Especially
Carissa and Carol
Jan and the Water Aerobics Class
TOPS 985
Wichita Area Romance Authors (WARA)
The Avalon loop

Chapter One

"Ouch! Fiddle!" the dark haired beauty exclaimed as she sat huddled among yards of white tulle.

A soft breeze rustled the leaves on the huge beech tree outside the window of the sewing room at Number 23 Hanover Square. It gently nudged a golden curl astray on the carefully coifed, lovely young miss diligently plying her needle beside her dark haired cousin.

Reproach filled Lady Margaret's eyes. "Do be careful," she cautioned. "You may get a spot of blood on the tulle and then—"

"Then I shall bloody well be done in," Louisa Elliott finished for her. "Really, Meg—"

"Grandmama said you must not call me that any longer," the blond admonished gently.

Louisa grimaced as she carefully eased the tulle along the gathering thread. "It will not do to wheedle me—*my lady*." The thread snapped and she exclaimed, "Bloody raspberries! By the gods I was never meant to ply a needle!"

"Take care, Louisa. What if Aunt Edwina had heard you." Lady Margaret blanched, "or Grandmama!" She stared at the cloud of sheer netting engulfing them. "Oh, why *did* you do it?"

Louisa studied the columbine yellow of her delicately featured cousin's hair, the dismay in the china blue eyes, the slight quivering of the dainty bottom lip. "I'm sorry I'm so clumsy, Meg." She scanned the inauspicious results of the Countess Tember's command that she fashion a gown. "How could Grandmama devise such a horrid punishment?"

"I know you never 'plan' these things. But after all my lessons, to not only tip your plate over the earl of Shrewsbury but to spill your lemonade on his lady." Lady Margaret shuddered.

Louisa swallowed her chagrin. "If only Grandmama hadn't given me that horrible lecture on decorum and social grace right before we went to the ball."

"Could you not recall even the tiniest portion of what we practiced?" Lady Margaret saw the slight twitch of her cousin's eye, a certain sign of embarrassment, and sighed.

"It doesn't do any good to talk about it," Louisa said bitterly. Her shoulders sagged dejectedly. At twenty she had proven a failure in society. "I am but a scapegrace."

"Then why do you persist in trying to please Grandmama?" Lady Margaret asked gently. "Would it not be easier to withdraw to Hamilton Manor?" she said wistfully.

"You've reason to wish me there," Louisa said tightly.

"But I don't." Meg reached across the tulle and gently squeezed her cousin's hand. "Believe me."

"I can't help but add luster to your star," Louisa answered bracingly. "Your grace and charm are beyond reproach while I—" She loosed a sudden chortle of laughter. "While hostesses set footmen to follow me and protect their guests."

Lady Margaret shook her head. "I don't see the humor."

"But if I don't laugh, I'll cry." Louisa smiled reassuringly then took up her needle once more.

A sudden thought caused Lady Margaret to pale. "You don't think Grandmama will make you wear this?"

"Now that would be a sight! Never fear," she hastened to reassure her easily alarmed cousin. "I'd be finished in the marriage mart if I did. Grandmama wouldn't risk dimming my chances further," she teased.

"Do be serious, Louisa." Lady Margaret sighed. "Grandmama may do as she has been threatening all season."

"Could she truly persuade some gentleman that I am the lady of his dreams," Louisa tossed back saucily. "Oh, Meg, you needn't gape as if I had blasphemed."

"But Grandmama *always* does what she says. How can you doubt it when you have been with her ever so much longer than I?

"Remember Captain Morris who used to call on Aunt Edwina? Grandmama said aunt could not marry him and she did not."

"Meg," Louisa said sharply, then conscious of her cousin's sensibilities, reconsidered her words. "You need only study me," she said instead, "to realize she cannot *always* succeed."

Lady Margaret could not deny that Louisa was forever falling into scrapes and social gaffes. "I have pondered that," she said slowly. "One would think that being only nine when you came to live with Grandmama you could not fail to be more—"

"Perfect," Louisa ended for her, a tinge of sarcasm beneath her rueful smile. "You're her great comfort, you know. With your delicate beauty and social sense." She clenched the tulle. "If only I wouldn't—wouldn't freeze when I attend those dastardly affairs."

"Now you have stuck yourself again," Lady Margaret cried.

Louisa looked down. "Now there is blood on it." She fought back the sudden threat of tears. "Isn't this just like me?"

"I shall fetch some water," Lady Margaret said, rising

gracefully. She quickly returned and began daubing at the spot.

Watching her cousin work, Louisa asked, "Isn't it odd that you have yet to receive an offer?"

"Well—yes. But Grandmama explained that gentlemen wait until the end of the season to speak," she offered naively. "It has been a huge relief for I have yet to meet a gentleman with whom I am—comfortable," Meg confided artlessly.

"Not even the marquess of Talbot?" Louisa teased.

Lady Margaret laughed. "At five and sixty?"

"The Viscount Bartone?"

"He is handsome I must admit. But far too fierce-looking. Who would you choose for a husband?"

"I spend far too much time trying not to trip over flounces and large-buckled evening shoes to contemplate faces," Louisa laughed.

"What will you do if Grandmama proposes a match for you?"

"I've never considered it." Louisa pushed a hand through her unruly curls. "You are the one who needs to be wary. The marquess's title is not above Grandmama's ambition." Her eyes danced mischievously.

"What of the duke of Hargrove?" She was instantly filled with regret at her cousin's dismay. From the beginning of the season Meg had shied away from the duke whose wealth and good looks had every eligible miss and mama plotting. "I daresay, his grace considers himself too high in the instep for you."

Lady Margaret blushed. "He has often danced with me."

"He has yet to even disdain to 'see me'," Louisa threw back.

Tears welled in Meg's eyes. She didn't dare reveal the reason for her aversion to the duke to Louisa, her most trusted confidant. "You don't think Grandmama would wish such a match for me?" she asked tremulously.

"You would have only to refuse him," Louisa said gently. She sighed inwardly, aware that her docile cousin would never be able to stand firm against the countess.

Lady Margaret stood with the towel and bowl of water. "The spot is gone. I'll put this away."

Louisa also rose and went to the window. She longed for Hamilton Manor and its solitude. *No one to laugh at or correct me—most of the time,* she thought.

A gust of wind waved the branch before her. "How large you've grown," she addressed the tree. "You were a sapling when we met." *Ten long years,* she thought, going back in time.

Countess Tember glowered and abruptly motioned to her young granddaughter. "Child, come forward. Stand up straight."

"Yes, Grandmama," nine-year-old Louisa answered in a quivering voice. Her parents' deaths in a coaching accident two weeks ago haunted her; increased her nervousness.

"You shall be in your Aunt Edwina's charge. On Sundays you shall recite your catechism to me and attend church." The countess frowned. "Can't you stand on both feet, child? Your training must have been very lax. Your mother was extremely foolish to have married beneath her."

Louisa clenched her fists hoping to keep back threatening tears. "Mother taught me very well."

"Dare you contradict me?" gasped the countess. "To your chamber until your manners improve."

Louisa hurried to the door. She looked back, longed to run to her grandmother, to be held tightly, and told that everything would be all right.

An answering scowl pressed her to depart. Blinded by

tears, Louisa ran out of the room, up the great stairs, and through the first door she came to—the sewing room.

How well I remember that first encounter. Louisa studied the leaves. *I have much to be grateful for, not the least of which is Meg. What a cold winter day it was when she arrived.* Once again Louisa slipped into reverie.

"Your cousin, Lady Margaret Hamilton, will be coming to live with us," Countess Tember imparted when Louisa was five and ten. "Your uncle—her father—died two days past of a fever." Her facade quavered slightly.

"My last child, my only son." She sighed and abruptly stiffened. "Lady Margaret shall have your bedchamber. Remove to the smaller one next to it." The countess paused.

"I trust you will be on your best behavior. You must strive to act like a Hamilton."

Dislike and jealousy reared their heads. These emotions grew during the week before her cousin's arrival. But upon meeting Lady Margaret, they melted away.

Louisa saw at once that the petite girl of four and ten was no adversary, only a grief-stricken figure much as Louisa had been upon her arrival. Instead of flinging out a challenge as she had planned, Louisa opened her arms. The younger girl came into them sobbing. At that moment, Louisa vowed to protect her from their grandmother's unbending sternness.

Lady Margaret's beauty, her grace and social aplomb could have embittered Louisa as much as Meg's constant refusal to go against what their grandmother wished. But Meg did her best to hide Louisa's transgressions. She understood the pain the countess's rebuffs caused, and provided solace.

Louisa flowered in her own way, becoming a pretty, self-assured young woman—except for the extreme nervousness that marked her every appearance in society.

"Poor Meg," Louisa said softly as she turned back to the heap of tulle. *If only she weren't such a gentle soul. If only I could make Grandmama see she only wants to be a squire's wife, peacefully raising her family in the country or a barrister's spouse responsible for home and hearth. Not part of the aristocratic world Grandmama wants for her.*

"How can Meg do so well in society when she fears it?" Louisa puzzled. "I'll never understand."

Lady Margaret paused in the doorway. "What don't you understand?"

"Everything," Louisa replied, smiling wryly. "Instruct me again what to do when going in to dinner at a ball." She sighed. "Perhaps we can forestall Grandmama's desperate measures."

"Be seated, Edwina. Stop fussing," Countess Tember commanded irritably. "This meeting must be completed before Lady Margaret and Louisa return." She looked over at the six ladies assembled at her bidding. Two were her sisters. The others were an assortment of the more influential matriarchs of the Hamilton and Hollace families.

"This matter is serious," the countess began. "We must deal with the problem of Louisa," she said in crisp condemnation.

"Mother . . ." Lady Edwina ventured timorously, only to bow her head when the countess scowled.

"You are all familiar with the problem Louisa presents. Far worse, Mary," she addressed her sister, "than your Portia. How is that child? Fine, I dare say," Countess Tember answered herself, "with the husband we secured for her."

"Twenty years older than Portia, if a day," Cousin Jane

Joan Vincent

whispered to her neighbor. "And coarse as Welsh wool."

Lady Edwina Hamilton clasped her hands tightly. Watching her mother and various aunts and cousins dispose of lives like one would sell fruit at the market distressed her. *Even if Portia was a buck-toothed, pox-marked miss, she deserved a better chance at happiness,* she thought.

The painful memory of the negative vote on Captain Morris was perseveringly pushed down. Lady Edwina wondered how Louisa would react to their arbitrary matchmaking. Of Lady Margaret's compliance she had no qualms. *Meg is extremely biddable, as I was*, she thought unhappily. *But Louisa?* A smile almost escaped.

"You know the chit's faults," Countess Tember said sternly. "What are your suggestions?"

Reprehensible silence fell.

"Come now. There must be someone we can foist her on," Countess Tember demanded.

"What of Cousin Jack's third son?" Lady Elizabeth, the countess's youngest sister proposed timidly.

"There is that young popinjay, Bradley," Cousin Jane offered. "His ilk is easily cowed."

"Or Medlock's Francis," Cousin Mary suggested.

The women fell silent; each mentally examined the various qualities of the nominated candidates.

"A more miserable lot I've never been forced to consider." Countess Tember's scowl deepened. "I suppose there's no hope for it."

Her long fingers tapped the delicate arm of her Windsor chair. "Jack's son has been marked for the Merville chit. A perfect match considering the addition it will bring to the estates." She smiled wan approval.

"It is common knowledge that Cousin Medlock has despaired of her Francis ever wedding," Mary began anew. "We could solve two, err, problems, so to speak."

The women exchanged meaningful glances.

Lady Edwina's heart sank.

"His age?" demanded the countess.

"Three and twenty."

"A fortunate number of years. What of his looks?"

"He is the young man who broke the Serves vase last Michelmas, Mother," Lady Edwina offered.

Cousin Jane coldly ticked off the gentleman's attributes. "You know the one. Broad of shoulder, tow headed—passable looked even if a bit too short in the calf."

"Isn't he a rather shy fellow?" asked one of the women.

"I've heard he wishes to buy a small estate and become a squire," another offered. "That would remove Louisa from society."

Countess Tember raised a finger to her chin, her eyes narrowed. "He was proposed for the Badley chit two years past, but her family wouldn't agree to it. Francis may suit tolerably well."

"Has Louisa met him?"

"She tripped him in the corridor that same Michelmas," Lady Edwina sighed. "And he tread on her flounce while dancing."

"There you have it. It could not be more suitable." The countess raised an eyebrow, signaling the end of the discussion. "Who has the most influence with this young man?"

"Lord Tenbury has guided him of late and Francis is very attentive to his mother," Mary assured her.

"Excellent. It shall be arranged." The countess ended the case without further thought. "Now for a more pleasant circumstance." A haughty smile curved her lips. "Lady Margaret has had offers from a viscount, an earl, and a marquess."

"Then why do we discuss her?" Cousin Jane snorted.

"Lady Margaret knows none of this. She has the looks and family to do better. With our help, she shall," Countess

Tember stated imperiously. "Her match shall be *the* triumph of the season."

Each lady looked to the other for a clue as to what gentleman the countess had decided to bring up to scratch.

Her sister began tentatively, "No one denies Lady Margaret is our best opportunity in years to improve the family fortunes, but surely a marquess is not to be lightly dismissed?"

"Nor was he. The match I propose has even greater consequence."

"Whom?" they asked as one.

"Hargrove," the countess said triumphantly.

"The duke of Hargrove? You can't mean it, Mother!" Lady Edwina said without thinking. "He has avoided all lures for the past ten years. And Margaret—I am certain she fears him."

"Nonsense," Countess Tember dismissed her concern.

"Is he amenable?" Cousin Jane demanded, irritated at the countess's triumph.

"It looks promising."

"Signed and sealed, I'd say," snorted her sister.

"As you all know, Hargrove's county seat marches beside Hamilton Manor. I have decided to make the most propitious use of that circumstance," the countess told them.

None dared to disagree.

"Prepare the tea, Edwina," Countess Tember said. She nodded condescendingly. "I know I may rely upon each of you to speak with your husbands to ensure our plans."

Lady Edwina fussed over the tea service and made certain all was arranged as her mother liked. Stepping aside to allow her to pour, she sighed heavily.

Lady Meg is fearful of the duke of Hargrove, Lady Edwina thought and was filled with dismay, which grew when her thoughts turned to Louisa. Despite the countess's determination, Lady Edwina was certain Louisa would not accept marriage with Francis Medlock with ladylike demureness, peaceful compliance, or expected gratitude.

"Do stop sighing, Edwina," Countess Tember reproved her.

Thinking of what was to come, Lady Edwina silently prayed, *Deliver us, O Lord.*

Chapter Two

"M' lord! M' lord!" Two young boys churned to a halt before the tall, velvet-coated gentleman strolling far from the usual paths in Hyde Park. Both spoke urgently, garbling the other's words.

"Silence!" An uplifted cane ensured it. "One of you speak." The gentleman tapped the oldest. "You."

"It's Louisa! You must help her for we'll all be cock a hoop if she isn't freed," he babbled.

The younger boy dared to tug at the elegant gentleman's cutaway jacket. "Come!"

A raised brow failed to rescue his velvet. Lord Hargrove pushed the offending hand away with the tip of his cane. "There is nothing I can do." He began to turn away.

More excited shouting and the patter of feet on the grass announced the arrival of a third child. "*Pwease* come sir," the little girl of five pleaded. She took a hold of his hand.

At this audacity, a good-natured laugh escaped Hargrove. Assured by a quick glance that the person he awaited hadn't yet arrived, he conceded and followed her.

"Is Louisa your dog?" he asked the children as they scampered before him.

"Dog!" hooted the boys, their concern fading in a gale of laughter.

The little girl blushed indignantly. "*Pway* no mind to them. It is their *fwault*."

Ambling along, Lord Hargrove was puzzled when the children halted beside a fallen tree. A lad was lying atop it, his eye to a knothole. In front of it stood two little girls clasping each other tightly and sobbing.

"The tree is hollow, m'lord," the eldest of the menagerie told the duke. "She's trapped inside it."

"How did the bloody animal get snagged? They usually are brighter," he noted frowning. When a strange, garbled sound answered his tap on the log, he added, "What an odd beast."

"She can hear you, m'lord," one of the lads explained. "I'd watch what I said," he gave a child-wise warning.

Hargrove sauntered to the end of the log where the young girls were clustered. Two definitely feminine feet thrashed about within the gapping mouth of the hollow trunk. Though taken aback, he said loudly, "No wonder it wasn't on a leash."

An unladylike tirade and a defiant kick answered. "John Paul?! Who is with you? Tell him to go away," came the muffled command from within the log. "Take care to watch the other children."

"We brought a gentleman, Cousin Louisa. He's going to free you," the lad shouted back.

"Brought a—" A loud thump sounded followed by a low moan.

The duke of Hargrove was hard-pressed not to laugh. Only the worried, tear-ridden mob about him compelled him to rein in the urge. "Silence," he commanded.

The little girls paled and sobbed with renewed vigor.

Hargrove crouched down before them. "I must hear Cousin Louisa if I'm to help her."

The red-eyed little ladies bobbed their heads jerkily then awkwardly sniffled into silence.

"It's Matt's doing. If he hadn't hit the ball—"

"It was because Alice is such a poor batman," Matt bristled. "She can't—"

"Gentlemen." The curt tone silenced them. The cricket bats lying to one side explained the probable cause of the situation. *It is an unlikely governess indeed,* he thought, *to treat a crew such as this to a cricket match. But why didn't she send one of them to retrieve the ball?*

John Paul's head drooped, chagrin brought a blush to his cheeks. "What should we do, m'lord?"

"Watch the other children," Hargrove repeated Louisa's command. He surveyed the pell-mell of petticoats and their owner's obvious displeasure. "If you would remain still, miss, I might be able to extricate you."

Hargrove appraised the shapely ankles as they waved a futile reply. "Perhaps I should take my leave?"

"Pwease, no," Amanda pleaded. "Miss Louisa *sounds* terrible but she isn't really. She will be in such *dreadful* trouble if great-grandmama should find out. Mama says—"

"Amanda," John Paul cut off his little sister, his youthful honor rising in defense of his favorite cousin.

The duke studied well-turned calves above sturdy shoes, and hazarded a guess at the governess's age. "Are you tired enough to remain still a moment?" The answering kick curved the corners of his mouth.

"Can you tell me what is snagged? Your skirt? Your jacket?" A true smile formed. "Or did you proved to be, err, a bit large? Should I send for someone to saw the tree apart?"

"I don't know what is caught," came the muffled snappish reply. "If I did I would free myself."

Hargrove's smile widened. "Then I must investigate. Lay quietly." He pushed her skirts aside, accidentally brushing a gloved hand against Louisa's leg. Her sharp kick against his arm drew an irritated grimace. He captured the trim ankles and pinned them down while he searched out the problem. Discovering that a large, jagged splinter had caught Louisa's jacket, Hargrove said, "Lie still while I pry loose the splinter that is holding you," he commanded. He released her ankles and took up his cane. A few jabs against the offending article broke it off. "That should do it, miss."

Louisa Elliott crept backwards in the log. Embarrassment rivaled with anger as her rescuer's hands look firm hold of her waist and set her firmly upon the ground. Brushing his hands away the instant her feet touched earth, she indignantly turned to face him. "That wasn't necessary."

"You forgot the ball," Matthew complained and was promptly silenced by a jab in his ribs from his older brother.

Hargrove could not resist. "Yes, thoughtless of you."

Louisa's color heightened further. Her eyes locked with his. Foreign warmth sprang to life. Then recognition struck her dumb.

Irritation covered the duke's concern as all color drained from her face. "You aren't going to faint, are you?"

With a trembling hand, Louisa brushed at the sawdust and cobwebs in her hair; tried to draw her wits about her. *Hargrove, of all men! Of all the foul luck.*

"I suggest that you send one of the children after the ball if this occurs again," the duke offered, unaware of the sharpness of his ingrained commanding tone.

Reminded of her grandmother, she said nervously, "I didn't want them to muss their clothing."

"Commendable," his lordship said loftily.

Color flooded across Louisa's face.

Gad, she's a pretty thing, he thought, suddenly bemused.

Louisa clenched her hands as mortification and anger raged in her. Yet a strange underlying emotion held her silent.

Yielding to an impulse, Hargrove deftly turned Louisa's back to him. "Let me remove the splinters from you jacket."

Louisa attempted to swing back only to find her long hair, dislodged from its pins by her struggle, caught fast on one of Hargrove's gold jacket buttons. "Now see what you've done," she scolded. She frantically tried to free her hair so she could move away from his increasingly disturbing presence.

"I did nothing," Hargrove answered indignantly. "Stand still," he cracked. He strove to untangle the silky brown strands from the button. The termagant smelled of wood dust and, as he leaned closer, orange blossoms.

Louisa closed her eyes. "This is ridiculous," she sighed.

The children, some crying, some excitedly offering instructions, agitatedly milled about the pair.

Visions of her grandmother's retribution sprang into Louisa's mind. She opened her eyes and strove for some control in the chaos. "Children, please, step back," she ordered.

They pressed closer as she turned, forcing her to brace a hand against Hargrove's broad, linen-covered chest. Her palms tingled at his strength and warmth; her senses reeled at the lure of spice and leather.

"Perhaps," she began vaguely, then stared up into his depthless eyes. "If you removed your jacket?" she suggested huskily.

Hargrove's gaze cradled Louisa. An indefinable exchange passed between them and she began to relax. She failed to see the darkening flame in his eyes as her gaze went to his lips. An unexpected longing filled Louisa. She sighed when he bent his head and feathered a kiss across her lips.

The brief contact commanded more. Both leaned forward

as their lips caught and held. When they drew back, they gazed at each other in questioning surprise.

John Paul drew himself to the full height of his two and ten years. "That was a—a dastardly act, m'lord." The lad drew a pocketknife from his breeches, snapped it open, and slashed the entrapped button from Hargrove's coat. He offered his arm to his speechless cousin.

"I—I am sorry—for—the button," Louisa stuttered and blindly accepted the boy's arm. With a last look, she allowed herself to be led away. The other children hastened to follow, leaving Lord Hargrove gaping after them in stunned silence.

"Of all the—" He left the thought unfinished, his eyes locked on the hastily retreating menagerie, and on Louisa's questioning glance back.

"*Mon seigneur. Mon Dieu! Votre veste!*" the smallish, dark man exclaimed at the hole in the velvet cutaway.

Hargrove snapped his gaze to the Frenchman. "An— accident," he said, and straightened his shoulders with an impassivity gained from years of being on display. "Your news?"

"*Le bateau arrive a l'heure.*"

"*Ne dites pas francaise,*" Hargrove ordered. He glanced about them. "We don't want to arouse anyone's suspicions."

"Late, aren't you, Mr. Forkman?" Countess Tember greeted the solicitor who had served her for over forty years.

He nodded with schooled contriteness. "Yes, my lady."

"Have you examined the matters I put before you?" she asked.

Adjusting his spectacles, the solicitor said, "The matter was simple. I handled the settlement of the estate for Louisa Elliott upon her parents' deaths. I contacted the Elliotts as you requested and they, as in the past, have declined to express an interest in what has been proposed for Miss Elliott."

"Speak plainly, sir. Will they give a dowry to the child?"

"No, my lady. Therefore I have taken the liberty of drawing up a document." Mr. Forkman handed over the parchment outlining a dowry settlement for Louisa.

"We shall see," her ladyship said, taking the paper. "Harrumph." She scowled. "I suppose it'll do."

"You are most generous, my lady. To me and to Miss Elliott," the solicitor murmured.

"Duty," she clipped. Countess Tember clasped her hands and peered sharply at Forkman. "What of the manor Francis Medlock wishes to own?"

"I've made arrangements for its purchase. It'll be yours in less than two weeks, my lady." Mr. Forkman squared his age-stooped shoulders. "May I speak?"

"Go on."

"I've known Miss Elliott for many years," he began tentatively, "and I can't think that she and Mr. Medlock shall suit. His nature is not adequate to deal with—"

"It isn't for you to *think*, Mr. Forkman. I know what is best for my granddaughter. Apprise me when the manor is mine."

The solicitor bowed tiredly. "Yes, my lady."

"The other matter?"

"I've investigated it. There is no possibility that the present Count Tember can challenge your right to dispose of Hamilton Manor as you see fit. It wasn't entailed and as Lady Margaret's guardian—"

"That's all," she dismissed him. "Begin drawing up the documents for dowry and marriage gifts from the duke of Hargrove."

Forkman straightened in surprise. "An agreement has been reached, my lady?"

"The matter is progressing." Countess Tember dismissed him. She rang her chair-side bell to hurry his hesitant departure.

Lady Edwina came silently into the salon. She nodded at Mr. Forkman as he withdrew. "Yes, mother?"

"I mean to call upon Cousin Medlock this afternoon. It'll please you to know that Louisa's future is assured. Have you prepared her for marriage?"

"Of—of course, mother," Lady Edwina answered. She lowered her gaze beneath the countess's sharp-eyed glance.

"We won't act too precipitously. That would cause undue scandal. But four weeks should suffice," the countess ruminated as she drew on her gloves.

"Four weeks?!"

"Before the announcement appears in the *Gazette*," Countess Tember snapped impatiently. "I'll also call on Lord Pattern. He is influential with his nephew, Lord Hargrove. Perhaps Lady Margaret's betrothal can be announced even sooner. The duke has been very attentive."

"He has only danced with Meg," Lady Edwina protested.

"His grace has taken pains to speak with Lady Margaret as well. Few young ladies have had that privilege." The countess halted at the door.

"I can't be easy until Lady Margaret is safely wed for fear of what rub that scapegrace Louisa will throw in the way of my plans. Lord Hargrove is too high in the instep to have noticed her thus far, but with marriage proposed he may take a keener interest in family. You must see that Louisa behaves properly."

Lady Edwina's shoulders sagged when her mother was out of sight. *How am I to prevent Louisa from being herself?*

Chapter Three

Lord Glynn Brice peered perceptively at the tall lithe man opposite him. "You are preoccupied this eve, your grace."

Lord Keane Patrick, duke of Hargrove turned his gaze from the empty hearth to his friend of many years. A wry grin teased the corners of his firm lips. "Your displeasure is noted, my lord," he returned the other's teasing formality. He waved languidly toward the fireplace.

"Does your Welsh spirit see anything in the ashes this eve?" Hargrove mocked.

"Ashes, my friend, are often more telling than flames," Lord Brice returned softly. His eyes narrowed as he recalled the duke's unusual distraction. "You met someone today. Someone who will be of more greater import in your life than Lady Angela Badden."

Irritated that he had been thinking of the "Cousin Louisa" in the park, Hargrove grunted, "It's fortunate for you that I tolerate your philosophic mutterings."

Lord Brice's gaze challenged him. "You met no one?"

"I think the Welsh mists have dampened your mind at

20

last," the duke said, his tone full of displeasure. He abruptly asked, "What do you think—is it time I wed?"

"You have not succumbed to Lady Badden's charms?" Lord Brice asked, arching a brow. "That was not your assignment."

Hargrove scowled; he was unwilling to discuss the task the War Office had set with the woman rumored to be his mistress. "A drink?" he said, motioning to the decanter, then poured and handed a goblet to Brice.

"I did meet someone today. Well, one cannot say 'meet.' Encountered is more apt. In Hyde Park near the rendezvous point. A governess, I think."

Lord Brice looked up with interest. "Think?"

"She was wedged in a hollow log." Hargrove sipped tentatively. "Got stuck trying to retrieve a cricket ball."

A smile bespoke Lord Brice's curiosity.

"I daresay she would make a capital player." Hargrove grinned openly. "Well-formed legs—for the running."

"Any other attributes meet with your approval?"

A sudden desire not to flaunt anything about the young woman hit Hargrove. "I could not say. Merely freed her and sent her on her way with the children." Hargrove drank deeply, refusing to meet Lord Brice's gaze.

"You mentioned marriage. Were you serious?" Lord Brice asked, slowly swirling the dark liquid in his goblet.

"What?" Hargrove drew his mind from challenging brown eyes that had met his flashing with anger instead of simpered pleasure; from the sweetness of her lips. "Oh, that. Countess Tember has let it be known she would welcome my suit."

Lord Brice cradled the stem of his glass. "Wealthy, but a touch on the aged side. I shan't approve, my boy."

"Lady Margaret Hamilton is neither poor nor old," Hargrove corrected with soft hauteur.

"Wealth. Youth. Beauty. Not small recommendations."
Lord Brice paused, studying his friend.

"But?" demanded Hargrove.

"Your Grace, why should I question it?" An impassive
smile lit Lord Brice's features. "She is sought by many, is in
perfect awe of your title and is certain to be easily molded to
your ways. The perfect duchess. What more need I say?" he
asked with unusual asperity.

"What more, indeed," Hargrove clipped. "You'll be late
for the soiree if you delay longer."

Lord Brice rose. A friendship of many years bound the
two men. Understanding the isolation brought on by rank
and wealth, he treated Hargrove with irreverent friendship.
In return, Glynn found his own enigmatic personality given
a rare comprehension. "You are in a rash mood." He set his
goblet on the elegant sideboard. "I counsel caution."

Their eyes met and held.

"It is noted."

"You grow pompous, Your Grace." Lord Brice smiled but
a hint of a frown shadowed his eyes. He bowed and silently
withdrew.

"Does Your Grace require anything?" the butler asked
from the doorway.

"No. Yes. Have my landau brought about," Hargrove
ordered curtly, champing against the unusual disquiet that
arose when Lady Margaret's beauty was replaced by
"Cousin Louisa's" image.

"Yes, Your Grace." The man bowed lowly.

A scowl marked Hargrove's handsome features. Above
average height, he was muscular without marring heaviness.
His clear blue eyes set off his fine aquiline nose and thick
brown hair, which tended toward blondness. Many read
strength in his features while failing to note the sensitivity.
He had been sickly as a child and deprived of the compan-

ionship of others near his age until he was sent to Oxford at six and ten.

It wasn't until his friendship with Viscount Brice that he became conscious of how he used an arrogant, over-bearing manner to cover the timidity caused my his over-protected, cosseted childhood. Or that he accepted the constant pandering of servants and friends as his due.

I shall have to apologize to Glynn, Hargrove thought. *And tell him the truth of the incident. Cousin Louisa is as skilled as he in denuding me of self-importance.*

Louisa.

A smile curved his lips; warmth filled his eyes. The tangle of dark curls, veil of cobweb, defiant thrust of chin belied by vulnerability tugged at his heart. He was vastly tempted.

Hargrove did not doubt she would welcome his attentions, even an alliance, once she knew who he was. But honor, as well as arrogance, had been ingrained. A naive young miss was not fair game.

No, he thought, *for once Glynn is wrong. She will play no part in my life.*

A light tap at her door sent Louisa scurrying back to her bed. She assumed a contrite forlornness. "Yes?" It faded as soon as she saw the delicate blond locks.

"Shh." Glancing fearfully back, Lady Margaret entered and eased the door shut. At her cousin's bedside she produced an apple and a large piece of cheese carefully wrapped in a napkin. "I thought you'd be hungry."

"I'm ravenous," Louisa laughed, gratefully accepting the bundle.

"Grandmama said she'll allow you out of your room on the morrow," Meg told her.

"If only Matthew had held his tongue." Louisa munched into the apple.

"Four days with only broth and bread is severe," Lady Margaret agreed sympathetically. "But Grandmama was almost overset by the incident."

"It was none of my doing. I ordered John Paul to tell the man to go away."

"Was it very dreadful being—being kissed by a stranger?" Lady Margaret shuddered. "I am certain I'd have swooned."

"If I ever meet his grace again . . ." Louisa began.

"His grace?" Lady Margaret's breath caught. "But you told Grandmama that you didn't know who—"

Louisa damned her blunder. "I'd no wish to cause an apoplexy."

"There are very few dukes in London this season," Lady Margaret mused.

"There'd be one fewer if I had my wish."

"Was it Lord Hargrove?" Her trembling hand gripped Louisa's. "Did he know you?"

"No, you silly rabbit. I'm too far beneath his touch to be noticed. He always looks 'through' me." Louisa's imitation of Hargrove's tone and manner teased a smile from Meg. "It was harmless. We were surrounded by the children."

Lady Margaret looked away. Silence filled the room. Then she said softly, "Grandmama spoke with me today. She—she said that Hargrove had expressed an—an interest."

Louisa studied her cousin. "Many think it'd be grand to be a duchess," she offered carefully.

"I couldn't bear it if I were forced to wed him." Meg burst into tears. "To contemplate marriage is dreadful enough but to—to him." Sobs prevented further words.

"Come, come, Meg." Louisa enfolded her in her arms as she had done when her cousin first joined the household. "I daresay it's natural to be fearful. But you mustn't hold a meaningless kiss against his grace. I once heard Grandmama say it was men's nature to—well, you know what I mean," she ended vaguely. "Besides, you can tell Lord Hargrove you dislike him."

"I couldn't do that." Lady Margaret daubed at a fresh spate of tears. "No, I'm lost if he asks for my hand." She sniffed loudly as she tried to regain her composure.

"You're right. My fears are—are nonsense. But—even his smile is so—so chilling."

Louisa flashed a bright smile. "When he learns I'm your cousin he shall bolt. If he doesn't, I'll tell him how low he stands in your opinion."

Lady Margaret gasped. "But then I'd be ruined. Pledge on your honor that you won't do that."

"As you wish," Louisa answered hurriedly, startled by the unusual vehemence of her gentle cousin. "Perhaps it'll not come to pass."

The certainty Meg felt in the countess's decision caused her to numbly shake her head. Then she recalled what she had overheard concerning Francis Medlock. *I dare not tell her,* she thought and quickly rose. "I'd best go to my room before Aunt Edwina comes."

"You mustn't worry, Meg," Louisa told her earnestly.

"It's foolish of me to become so overset." She forced a light laugh. "Grandmama wouldn't wish the match if it weren't for the best." Meg sighed, and then brushed her cousin's cheek with a kiss. "Sleep well, Louisa."

After finishing the apple, Louisa blew out the bedside candle, wrapped an arm about her pillow, and snuggled down into the featherbed. "Well your grace, you shall not wed Meg if she is unwilling," she bravely whispered. But for all her bravado, Louisa trembled at the thought of Lord Hargrove whose handsome face had oft been in her thoughts the four days past.

On the morrow I'll be free of this room, she thought, forcing her mind away from the perplexing, haunting emotion evoked by Hargrove's lips. *On the morrow I'll be free of thoughts of the duke.*

"I can't stress enough the danger such a situation could prove to your reputation," the Countess Tember ended her admonition to Louisa. "You are never again to dismiss the children's nannies or I'll instruct Jane and Mary to refuse you the children."

"Yes, Grandmama," Louisa said, concealing a frown.

"It's good to see you properly penitent." The countess congratulated her handling of the matter. "I'd no wish to impose such a severe restriction," she said, unbending slightly. "Especially at this time."

Her tone raised Louisa's eyes.

"You're in fine looks today, my dear. Excellent." Countess Tember paused, suddenly uncertain. "Nonsense," she muttered, casting aside doubt.

"Do you recall the young gentleman who stayed with us at Hamilton Manor last Michelmas—Francis Medlock?"

Puzzled, Louisa said, "Yes."

"Young Medlock will call this morning."

An unpleasant premonition formed. "But," Louisa began carefully, "you forbade him your presence when he broke—"

"Nonsense. The young man was merely nervous," the countess said impatiently. "Do make him welcome.

"But Edwina explained that to you already. Be off to the salon. I'll join you after he arrives."

Louisa bobbed a quick curtsy. She hastened from the sitting room and swept down upon her aunt.

"Aunt Edwina, what is it Grandmama believes you've explained about Mr. Francis Medlock?"

Distress washed across Lady Edwina's features. Her eyes

sought the embroidery work in her lap. "Why—I—I failed to mention he is to call this morn."

Louisa took her hand. "What is the reason for his visit?"

"My lady. Miss Elliott." The butler Grimes commanded their attention at the door. "Mr. Medlock," he announced and stepped aside.

Lady Edwina stood, a nervous smile of relief on her lips. "Good morn, sir."

Francis Medlock stammered a greeting; his stocky form an apologetic hulk. He tightened his grip on his beaver hat as the butler took hold of it, briefly struggled, and then realizing his error, allowed Grimes to bear it away. He blushed deeply. "I—I didn't think—"

Louisa compassionately strove to rescue him. "It's quite understandable, Mr. Medlock. Please be seated."

"Uh, why—why yes," Francis stammered. He stepped forward and tripped on the edge of the carpet.

Louisa took his arm with a comforting smile. "Perhaps you wish to sit with Lady Edwina." She led him to the settee and nudged him to sit. Taking a chair opposite, she sat silently waiting.

A look to her aunt revealed Lady Edwina's profound interest in her embroidery. Francis, she found, had just as avid an interest in the Tree of Life pattern in the Aubusson carpet beneath their feet.

"Is the morning pleasant, Mr. Medlock?" she threw out.

He jerked to attention. "What? Oh. Ah, yes, I suppose it is," Francis answered, nervously.

Silence again took root.

Lady Edwina stirred. She cleared her throat. "How is your mother?"

"Quite well. Good health, actually." Francis looked from one to the other. Noticing Louisa's curious stare he recalled what he had been badgered into and blushed deeply.

"Francis, how good to see you once again," the Countess Tember greeted the hapless young man.

"My—my lady," he gulped and struggled upright, unsuccessfully attempting a gracious bow.

The countess took his hand as he awkwardly straightened. "It's been much too long since you called. Do not stand, lad. Sit. There," she said pointedly, "next to Louisa."

A deep blush crawled from below Francis's crushed cravat to his hair line. He paused when he was half seated and then jerked upright. "A—a pleasure to see you," he murmured. "But must go," he said with unusual determination. "An appointment."

Louisa smiled with warm relief. "Then you must go at once."

"But you can't bolt like this." Countess Tember laid a hand on the young man's arm. "You *will* stay a bit longer."

Francis Medlock met her gaze briefly, then sank down next to Louisa. He glanced up, and realizing Countess Tember was still standing, bolted upright once again.

The countess smiled, nodded at him to sit as she retook her seat. "It is a beautiful day, Mr. Medlock."

"Yes, my lady."

"You've your own phaeton and pair?" the countess asked.

"Yes, my lady."

"Louisa has been indisposed. A drive would be most beneficial," she commanded.

"I'd be—be honored if you would go driving with me, Miss Elliott," Francis stammered, his eyes on the rug.

Louisa tossed her grandmother an angry reprove. "I mustn't keep you from your appointment."

"Call for Louisa this afternoon." Countess Tember stood.

"I—I may—yes." Medlock lurched to his feet and bowed. "At three," he said and bolted from the salon.

"Grandmother, how could you?" Louisa demanded.

"How could I what, my dear?"

"It's perfectly clear Mr. Medlock had no wish to be here, much less take me for a drive."

"Young men are shy when their affections are engaged."

Louisa's mouth momentarily sagged open. She sought her aunt's gaze but the other refused to meet hers.

"Mr. Medlock has asked for your hand in marriage," the countess said in a hard voice. "Naturally I felt you should become better acquainted before I gave my consent. You'll see Mr. Medlock daily. He'll escort us in the evening."

Louisa's stomach gave a sickening lurch. "I've no wish to wed Francis Medlock."

"My solicitor, Mr. Forkman has seen to the necessary papers. *I* shall provide your dowry."

"But Grandmama—" Louisa clenched her hands, her eyes imploring Lady Edwina to speak.

"You're not yet of age, Louisa." Countess Tember appeared to tower over her granddaughter though in truth she was much smaller. "I've provided for you for many years as your guardian. You will obey me and wed Francis Medlock."

Chapter Four

"I'm on a cart from Newgate prison slowly approaching the hangman's noose at Tynburn," Louisa forlornly told Lady Margaret a week after Francis's first morning call. "If only there was some way to escape."

"Perhaps Mr. Medlock will cry off—"

"Gentlemen aren't permitted to do so. Besides, Francis wouldn't dare defy Grandmama. He's so meek. Sometimes I could shake him!"

"Then tell him you'll not wed him. After all, you advised me to do that," her cousin answered softly.

Louisa scowled. "It's not as easy as that," she admitted. "If I were one and twenty—but it's no use to dwell on it. I must convince Grandmama that Francis and I don't suit."

Shaking her head, Meg sighed. "At least you know your fate. Grandmama hasn't said anything about Lord Hargrove."

Louisa didn't hear her. "If only Francis weren't so much like me. Putting him in an unpleasant situation with Grandmama would be heartless. It isn't his fault he can please no one," she mused sympathetically.

Louisa's eyes brightened. She cocked her head. "What if I were deathly ill and begged Grandmama to refuse the match?"

"She'd only summon a surgeon," Meg said, absentmindedly unraveling the edge of the blue ribbon about her dainty waist.

Hearing the long-case clock in the corridor strike eleven, Louisa stood. "I'd best fetch my hat and gloves. I'll spare Francis an interview with Grandmama by meeting him at the door." She paused.

"Would you care to go driving with us?"

"I can't," Meg answered sadly. "Lord Banfry and Sir Pomfret are to call this morn."

I'll have to do something about Meg, Louisa thought as she skipped down the grand central staircase in the entry hall.

"I'll get it, Grimes," Louisa told the butler when she heard the door knocker thud against the great main door. "Tell Grandmama and Aunt Edwina I've gone with Mr. Medlock."

Years of Miss Elliott's impropriety reasoned against arguing further but didn't forestall his grimace. "Yes, miss."

To spare Francis that look, Louisa waited until the butler walked away before opening the door.

The tall gentleman before her arrogantly arched a brow.

Recognizing the athletic form, Louisa gasped and stepped back. Her reticule slipped from her hand.

Lord Hargrove casually retrieved the treacherous purse with his cane. He held it out.

A deep blush rose to Louisa's startled features. She snatched the reticule only to find her hand enclosed in a strong grip.

"Is that a proper thank you?" he asked stepping inside and drawing her close.

Louisa noticed the rakish angle of his hat, the glint in his blue eyes. Her heart skipped a beat. "Thank you, my— your—" She watched him raise her hand to his lips, trembled when he kissed it.

"Perhaps," he tightened his hold, "I'll forgive you—this time."

Anger surged through Louisa at these highhanded words. She jerked her hand free and made to shut the door in his face.

The duke thrust his cane into the breech.

"How dare you?" Louisa bristled from the other side.

Amazement tightened Hargrove's jaw. He stared through the cane's width crack. "Is the countess at home?" he asked coldly.

"Your manner is most ungentlemanly, but then *that*'s no surprise."

His pleasure at seeing her, the surprising joy that surged through him, began to recede. "Cousin Louisa—"

"Miss Elliott to you, Your Grace," Louisa reprimanded with false bravado.

"Then you *do* know who I am."

"Of all the pretentious, overbearing—"

Hargrove stiffened. "Your manners have been shockingly neglected, Miss Elliott. I'll be forced to speak with the—" Her sudden whiteness sent an indefinable weakness through him. Perplexed, Hargrove drew upon his arrogance.

"Open this door and I'll not mention your behavior."

Louisa blanched. She slowly backed away from the door.

Hargrove tapped his cane on the floor as he sauntered into the hall. "See that I am announced to Lady Margaret Hamilton," he ordered curtly.

"Why do you wish to see Meg?"

"I see it isn't just my person you disrespect." Hargrove smiled, the humor of the scene overcoming him. When Louisa reached out and touched his hand, his heart leapt.

Louisa reeled from a melee of conflicting emotions at the contact. She dropped her hand. "Lady Margaret doesn't wish to see you."

"She doesn't know I called."

"Nor does she wish to know it," Louisa clipped, barring his way. "Leave at once."

"I *shall* see Lady Margaret."

I'll have you. The unbidden thought thoroughly startled the duke.

Louisa steeled herself against the flash in his blue eyes. *Eyes like the sea; eyes to drown in.* She forced herself to meet his challenging gaze. A peculiar stirring weakened her angry determination. She sensed a like change in Hargrove; saw his gaze take on the same cast as when he had kissed her. A sudden weakness struck her knees.

"Louisa? With whom are you speaking?" the countess called from the upper reaches of the staircase.

Whirling about to see where her grandmother was, Louisa offered a hurried prayer of thanks that she hadn't yet seen Lord Hargrove. She looked back to the duke and saw a glint of amusement in his eyes. Panic washed all color from her features.

Concerned, Hargrove reached for her.

The jingle of harness and the clop of hooves caught Louisa's ear. She looked past the duke through the open door. Francis Medlock was reining his phaeton and pair to a halt. "Francis is here, Grandmama."

Hurrying around Hargrove, Louisa brushed against him in her haste. Unaware that he had set his cane at an angle, her foot caught. She began to fall.

Hargrove caught Louisa, helped her regain her balance. The consternation in her eyes was a puzzle. That she was the countess's granddaughter shocked him.

Wrenching from his grip, Louisa blocked out her embarrassment. She grabbed hold of the doorknob and pulled it shut behind her with all her might. She swore in frustration at the wrench of her skirt as it caught in the door.

Opening the door, Hargrove grinned down at her. "Allow me," he said, bending and freeing the material. He straightened; a boyish impishness warmed his eyes and erased his habitual hauteur. "You have an affinity for wood, Cousin Louisa. At least my jacket fared better this time."

Louisa choked back a retort and bolted to Medlock's phaeton.

Francis's unease grew as he watched Lord Hargrove speak with Louisa. He saw that the duke still stood watching them.

"Help me," Louisa commanded thrusting up her hand when she reached the side of the phaeton. "At once."

"But shouldn't we—I mean, isn't that the duke of—"

"Must I mount by myself?" she threatened.

"Oh, my, no." Francis awkwardly tied off the reins and jumped down. Stumbling when he landed, he apologized and handed her up, only to step on her skirt.

"Must you be so clumsy," Louisa scolded, her gaze cast back to Hargrove's amused stance as she twitched her skirt free. Settling into the seat, Louisa saw Medlock's blush.

Why did I say that? she asked, realizing she sounded like her grandmother. Looking back as they drove off she saw the door was now shut. She sighed and glanced at Francis. He sat stiffly, whiteness about his mouth. Her mortification deepened.

"Your Grace," Countess Tember exclaimed upon finding the duke of Hargrove unattended in her entry hall. "Where is Grimes? He shall be severely—"

Hargrove bowed formally. "No, my lady."

She stiffened slightly. "Did you encounter Louisa?"

"No one, my lady."

The countess smiled tightly. "If only Louisa resembled her cousin, Lady Margaret, in *some* way," she continued. "But let us be comfortable." Countess Tember took his arm.

"Grimes," she ordered the startled butler when they encountered him, "tell Lady Margaret to come to the Oriental Salon at once.

"It is *such* a pleasure to receive you, Your Grace," she smiled with hidden triumph as they entered the ornately decorated salon. A massive red dragon carving above the fireplace stared back with cold Hamilton pride.

"I have been remiss in not calling sooner, my lady," Hargrove apologized. "Had I known you possessed two lovely granddaughters—"

"You have no need to waste compliments on Louisa," Countess Tember said with a harsh trill. "She is to be betrothed."

Lord Hargrove nodded, surprised to find something crimped about his heart at this news. His gaze traveled over the richly carved dragon, gazing down with open jaws. He was reminded of the countess and then of Lord Brice's prediction.

Countess Tember preened at what she took to be admiration. "It is lovely isn't it? It is after the Oriental flavor of the rooms at Brighton. The prince is the 'First Gentleman' of Europe; who can fail when guided by his taste. I understand you are oft his guest at Brighton."

"Yes, my lady. Any style tastefully done is pleasing," he murmured noncommittally.

"Lady Margaret has such exquisite taste. She shall be such an asset—why, here you are, my dear."

Meg sank into a deep curtsy. "Good morn, Your Grace."

Hargrove took her hand, admired her fragile beauty. He could not help contrasting it with her cousin's. "Your gown is extremely becoming, my lady," he said in an effort to ease the distress he saw in her eyes.

"You are kind, Your Grace," Meg murmured, gaze downcast.

Countess Tember motioned the pair to a dragon claw-footed settee with a hint of a frown on her features.

Hargrove chatted easily of common things but Lady Margaret contemplated her hands and gave monosyllabic answers. Despite the countess's grimaces and desperate attempts to aid the conversation, Hargrove soon made to leave.

Unsuccessful in achieving a commitment for the duke's next call, the Countess Tember bade Lady Margaret to remain in the salon and walked with Hargrove into the corridor. "My granddaughter is fittingly in awe of you," she explained, "and of the great honor your visit accords her. Undoubtedly this caused her unusual reticence this morn."

"Lady Margaret needs no defense, my lady," Hargrove told her. He condemned himself a fool for having accepted the lure of Hamilton Manor in contemplating marriage.

"I may be from London for some time. Estate business," he told her. "Till next we meet." He bowed again and strode away.

Countess Tember clenched her hands as his strong stride carried him from her grasp.

The doubtful yet hopeful gleam hovering on Lady Margaret's features melted into controlled fear when her displeased grandmother stalked back into the salon.

"You are never to display such social ineptness again," she said, her voice cracking like a whip. "Every morn you'll take breakfast in my chamber. We shall practice proper conversation—questions and replies."

"Yes, Grandmama," Meg answered weakly.

"A man wants respect and admiration, not simpering silence," she said angrily. "You are fortunate to be considered by a man as young, handsome, and esteemed as the duke."

"But—" Meg began hesitantly.

The countess's sharp glare cut the challenge. "What?"

"Nothing, Grandmama," she answered tiredly.

The countess studied her granddaughter closely and saw she was very pale. "Aren't you feeling well this morn?"

"A touch of the headache," Lady Margaret said with relief.

"I should have known. Here I've been upsetting you with a needless scolding. Go to your room. I'll send Edwina to you," she said with starched kindness.

"But," Countess Tember added when Meg had reached the door, "we'll breakfast together every other morn." Then more kindly, "You'll enjoy being a duchess, my dear."

"Yes, Grandmama." Meg hurried down the corridor before the tears could betray her.

Lord Brice stared impassively at Hargrove. They had met at White's several hours earlier and the viscount had watched his friend consume two bottles of port, a common quantity for the day, but not for the duke. Hargrove's mood had worsened with each bottle consumed.

"In a rare temper," Brice noted archly. "Lady Badden?"

Hargrove looked up accusingly.

"You have seen your young scapegrace again."

"She is the granddaughter of the Countess of Tember."

"How fortunate." Brice raised his glass in mock salute. "To Lady Margaret, your bride."

"Miss Louisa Elliott," he corrected. "She is to be betrothed to Francis Medlock," Hargrove added disgustedly.

"Medlock?" Brice raised a brow appraisingly. "Isn't that the chap whose team became ensnarled on Rotten Row a week past."

"The same."

The viscount folded his hands piously. "You fear defeat at his hands? Is Miss Elliott oblivious to your perfection?"

"She loathes me." Refreshing his glass he continued, "Considering Countess Tember's aristocratic greedy bent I find it difficult to believe she countenances such a match. She must approve because of her affection for Miss Elliott."

Brice smiled. "The wisdom of Socrates."

"You think otherwise?" Hargrove demanded belligerently.

"Countess Tember's 'kind' heart is well-known."

"Harrumph."

"To avoid a battle one would lose is wise. Besides, Lady Margaret has title, wealth—and is far superior in looks to Miss Elliott," Lord Brice baited.

"You have never seen—"

"On the contrary," Lord Brice countered. "Miss Elliott accompanies her cousin everywhere. I am surprised you had failed to note that." He smiled at Hargrove's chagrin. "Ask Lady Shrewsbury."

"Shrewsbury—" Hargrove's eyes widened at recalling a scene caused by spilled lemonade. "Louisa is the scape-grace?"

Lord Brice nodded and rose. "Let us attend the Landley's ball. You must wish to smile upon Lady Margaret."

Lord Hargrove glowered but followed without objection. Louisa would be there.

Chapter Five

"**Y**ou needn't remain at my side all evening, Francis," Louisa told the nervous young man standing attentively behind her chair at the far end of her aunt's ballroom. "Go and join the gentlemen in the card room."

Casting a fearful glance about for Countess Tember, Francis hesitated long enough to show he was tempted.

"Do go." Louisa smiled to cover her impatience.

"It wouldn't be gentlemanly."

"Francis, I wish to be alone," Louisa said adamantly.

Young Medlock recognized that tone. "Of course." He bowed perfunctorily and left.

Oh, Francis, she sighed silently. *Are you as wretched as I?* She heard Lady Margaret's tinkling laughter. A glow of relief filled her; her cousin's happy demeanor was a welcome change. She rose and joined Meg.

"You are unattended? But Mr. Medlock is so conscientious—"

"I told Francis to go to the card room," Louisa answered impatiently.

"But he dislikes gambling."

"How do you know that?" Louisa puzzled, then dismissed the question. "It's good to see you smiling again."

"It's your doing," Meg told her conspiratorially. "I was *horrid* to Lord Hargrove this morn. It must have succeeded, for the hour is growing late and he has yet to come." She clasped Louisa's hand.

"I haven't enjoyed an evening for ever so long." She flicked her with a fan in mock irritation at Louisa's inattentiveness. "At what are you staring?"

Louisa started. "Oh, nothing," she prattled nervously. "Could you fetch Francis, Meg? I'm getting a headache."

Suspicion flared across Lady Margaret's gentle features. Her cousin never suffered from the common malady. "Couldn't I fetch something cooling?"

Louisa took hold of her cousin's hand. "Just bring Francis. Do hurry," she added, sinking into her chair and posing with a hand to her head.

Lady Margaret hesitated. "You'll remain here?" A pain-filled grimace convinced her to go.

Louisa sighed with relief and swung a searching glance over the crush near the doors where the butler had stood in the early hours of the ball announcing the guests.

As she feared, she spied Lord Hargrove's tall figure, striking in full evening dress. The form-fitting white breeches and royal blue cutaway jacket suited him admirably. Lord Brice stood by his side like a shadow.

"Whatever Meg meant by 'being horrid' wasn't enough," Louisa muttered. She tapped her fan thoughtfully against the skirt of her high-waisted gown. *I must convince Lord Hargrove to depart immediately. And I mustn't be seen by Grandmama.* Pushing aside fear, Louisa worked her way through the crowd toward the duke.

Hargrove, surrounded as usual by the loveliest and most

noted ladies of the *ton*, was listening with bored attention to some jest by Lady Jersey when Lord Brice nudged him.

"Miss Elliott approaches," the viscount murmured with a nod in her direction.

Nonchalance turned to longing at sight of the determined young miss, not unattractive with her heightened coloring and emerald green gown. Realizing Brice was watching him, Hargrove strove to collect his wits and assumed an uninterested mein.

There was an unconscious moving aside as Louisa made her way through the crush. More than one lady had had a flounce torn or her ribbons hopelessly tangled in previous encounters. A few noted that she was walking with a new grace.

Louisa halted before the duke. "Lord Hargrove," she said, demanding his attention more sharply than she wished.

A languid gaze greeted her. "Miss Elliott, good eve," Hargrove said with feigned hauteur while he strove to gain control of his port-wracked mind and suddenly pounding heart.

"May I speak with—you—" She stumbled mentally, suddenly conscious of Lady Jersey's condemning glare.

"But you are."

A twitter ran through the throng.

"Miss Elliott, delighted so see you," Viscount Brice said at her side with a reproving glance at his friend. "We met at Lady Montague's soiree."

"Good—good eve, my lord." Louisa wrestled to handle the interruption gracefully. Her blush deepened, enhancing her beauty.

A frown curved Hargrove's lips at his friend's interference. "I see Lady Marriane, Brice. Didn't you wish to speak with her?" he asked pointedly.

"Did I?" Brice turned an impassive gaze on him. "I was about to ask Miss Elliott's hand for the allemande." He turned back to her with a warm smile.

Louisa blanched at the thought. "Lady Marianne is much the better dancer. Truly. I must speak with his grace."

"I'll concede only if you promise the next quadrille."

Lord Brice's soft voice calmed her fears; his steady gaze removed the unsettling effect of the curious stares.

"If you wish," she murmured gratefully.

"Later, then." He kissed her hand before taking leave.

Turning to Hargrove, Louisa was struck by his deep frown. "If only you were the gentleman Lord Brice is," she blurted.

Unfeigned surprise at this lack of respect replaced his assumed hauteur. "Truly?"

"Can't we speak privately, Your Grace?" Louisa asked, edging closer as she grew more conscious of stares. Then she heard her grandmother's voice.

"You must leave at once," she whispered urgently. "Else Grandmama shall entrap you into a match."

"You mistake the matter, Miss Elliott," the duke bristled. "No one 'entraps' a Hargrove."

"Don't be so—so addlepated," Louisa snapped. "Please leave."

"I came to dance with Lady Margaret and I'll not leave until I've done so." Instead of being pleased by her growing agitation, Hargrove found he wished to ease it. "The allemande is beginning, Miss Elliott. Let us—"

Anger exploded within her at his obtuseness. "Don't be ridiculous." She hurried a few steps away and then whirled back to escape the Countess Tember.

A footman bearing a tray of champagne-filled goblets had no warning of this sudden change of direction. He paused to offer the duke a glass.

Louisa glanced over her shoulder to check the Countess Tember's whereabouts. She collided with the servant and sent the tray arcing into the air.

The footman watched in speechless horror as it hung motionless for long seconds and then tumbled down, spilling the goblets' contents over the august figure of the duke of Hargrove.

The dancers, even those gossiping at the far end of the ballroom paused at the clanging, tinkling call of disaster.

Rigid hauteur held the champagne-fragranced Hargrove from outward demonstration of displeasure. He raised his hand to an inner pocket and slowly removed a fine Irish linen handkerchief. Daubing at his face, he took a deep breath before approaching Louisa who stood frozen in place. "I erred, Miss Elliott. I should have—"

"What *have* you done, Louisa?" the Countess Tember's infuriated tone cut through the binding spell of catastrophe.

Louisa, her cheeks bone-white, an ashen hue about her lips, whirled away. Her face crumpled in an effort not to yield to tears as she rushed through the crowd.

The countess brushed at Hargrove's soaked coat sleeve with her kerchief. "Your Grace, my humblest apologies. Louisa's behavior is inexcusable."

Hargrove brushed her hand aside. "Excuse me, my lady."

"Your Grace," Lady Margaret sank into a deep curtsy before him. "It was an accident, Your Grace. Louisa'd never do it on purpose. Pray, forgive her," she pleaded.

Taken aback by her evident fear, Hargrove hastily took her hand. "My lady, please rise. The footman merely slipped," he said loud enough for those listening. "Didn't you, good fellow?" he questioned the young man who was hurriedly retrieving broken glass.

"What, Your Grace?" he asked, jumping to attention.
"Whatever you say, Your Grace," he gulped.

"Collins, you are dismissed," Lady Landley announced.

"Yes, my lady." He bowed dejectedly, then continued his
task.

"Collins, is it?" Lord Brice's soft voice startled the footman as he stood with the tray full of broken glass. "Call at
his grace's residence in the morn."

A nod assured the footman he had heard right but before
he could speak the viscount turned back to Hargrove. With a
hint of a smile Brice inspected the duke. "I've ordered my
coach."

"Most gracious of you, Glynn," Hargrove attempted to keep
his voice light. "You will excuse me, Lady Landley. Ladies.

"Lady Margaret, may I call upon you in the morn?"

She paled, relief and dread mixed. "Of course, Your Grace."

"You've done it," Lady Landley crowed congratulations to
the countess when Hargrove was out of sight. "How fortunate you are, my dear," she smiled at Lady Margaret.

"Louisa's future shall be settled on the morrow. Medlock,
you may take us home," the countess ordered the young man
who had hurried to the scene.

"But Miss Elliott?" he quaked.

"She bolted, Mr. Medlock. Now you understand why a
retired setting is best for my granddaughter."

"Will your coach never come?" Hargrove demanded. He
had refused to re-enter Lady Landley's when the delay grew
lengthy.

"What did the Hamilton chit mean-sinking to the floor
and pleading? As if I'd harm her cousin," he scoffed angrily.

"At least it was champagne—fitting for a duke, no?" Lord
Brice said softly.

Hargrove gave him a hard look, then stalked into the

deeper shadows of the long, porticoed entrance. *Why did she have to run away like that?* he thought, battling an anger that had no clear direction.

A stifled sob halted his steps. Listening intently, the duke detected its direction. He spied a woman behind a pillar a few feet ahead.

"The coach is here, Hargrove," Lord Brice announced.

"Coming." Hargrove swung about. A second sob nagged at his heart. "By Hecate," he swore under his breath.

"Wait a moment," he told the viscount and strode back into the house. He returned a few moments later with a pale green evening cloak trimmed in royal ribbons. "What are you waiting for," Hargrove clipped, swinging into the coach.

The viscount joined him, a questioning glance at the cloak.

"Say nothing," Hargrove threatened, then to the driver, "Halt at the outer gates." When the driver did so he told the viscount, "I'll be back shortly." With the cloak in hand, he jumped down and disappeared in the direction of the house.

Quick, quiet steps brought Hargrove undetected to the far end of the Landley portico. Assured that the footmen were occupied with gossip, the duke slipped through the shadows to the figure leaning against one of the white columns.

"Your cloak," he offered softly. When Louisa turned to him in the shadow, he could see the tear-stained faced, unbearably vulnerable. He swallowed the sudden lump in his throat. "Come, Lord Brice awaits us. We'll take you home."

Louisa had bolted from the ballroom in complete humiliation, certain of failure. She didn't move despite wanting to run from this man. The gentle strength in his voice filled her with a calm security she hadn't experienced since her parents' deaths. Louisa walked past the cloak he held and buried her face in his fine lawn blouse, absorbing the solace unknowingly offered.

Hargrove trembled. He tenderly draped the cloak about her shoulders and rested his hands on them. An excitement far deeper than other encounters with ladies on shadowed porticoes had ever produced shot through his veins. It was tempered by the completely unexpected desire to protect her. He slowly slid his hands down her back, gently enfolded her in his arms.

A loud guffaw from a footman brought Hargrove back to reality. Longing to prolong the moment and yet knowing it was impossible, the duke gently drew back. "Lord Brice awaits us."

The words broke the spell holding Louisa. Stiffening, she glanced about in wordless question.

"It'd be best to go unnoticed, Miss Elliott."

Permitting him to take her hand, Louisa followed.

"Keane?" The viscount called as he stepped away from the coach. He summed up the pair approaching him hand in hand, saw Louisa withdraw hers in obvious confusion.

"May I hand you in?" he asked.

Louisa hesitated, then accepted his hand with a mute nod. Seated, she clenched her hands and prayed neither would speak. The last thing she recalled clearly before Hargrove told her that the viscount awaited, was the angry visage of her grandmother. She wrapped her arms tightly about herself foreswearing the comfort and warmth of Hargrove's touch. The rhythm of his heart's rapid tattoo.

A short time later Grimes shut the door of Number 45 Hanover behind Miss Elliott, his expression a mixture of disapproval and surprise when he saw that the duke of Hargrove had escorted her.

"That's all," Louisa dismissed the butler, knowing he would remain at attention until she retired. *Keane* she thought at she mounted the stairs. *The viscount had called Hargrove Keane.* She rolled the name over her tongue. "Keane." Had he held her because he cared? Was it her imagination?

"I'm going mad," she said. "And I've failed Meg."

Sounds of a barouche and four sounded outside the house.

"Grandmama," Louisa whispered and dashed up the stairs, halting only when she was certain she was out of sight.

"Not another word about Louisa," Countess Tember's voice crackled angrily. "Be happy that the duke is so smitten with you that he is willing to overlook her behavior. Remember that when he calls in the morn."

"Yes, Grandmama. Only Louisa did not mean to—"

"Enough! It is unlike you to challenge me." The countess's shoulders slumped. "To bed with you."

"Yes, Grandmama," Lady Margaret murmured. She dutifully brushed her grandmother and aunt's cheeks with a kiss. Assured of Louisa's return by the light beneath her cousin's door she fled to the safety of her own chamber.

In the entry hall Grimes awaited his mistress's orders.

"Has Miss Elliott returned?"

"Moments before you, my lady. Unharmed," he added at Lady Edwina's questioning gaze.

"You may go, Grimes. Edwina, send her to me."

Left alone the Countess Tember sighed, her hand heavy on the balustrade. *So far to have come*, she thought, carefully working her way up the stairs. *From a plain miss to a countess. My Tember, my husband.* Tears welled at the thought of the uncaring fop who had inherited the Hamilton earldom.

Better shall be had. Lady Margaret will wed Hargrove. The Hamiltons will have a duchess. The thought warmed her.

And Louisa? Countess Tember hardened her heart. *She shall learn as Edwina did that family always comes first.*

Chapter Six

"Good morning, Grimes," Hargrove said as he strode into the countess's entry hall with determined cheerfulness early the next morning.

"Come along Medlock, don't hang back," he called to his reluctant companion whom he had dragged from bed a short time earlier. "We'll await the ladies in the Oriental Salon," he tossed at the butler.

"But Your Grace, it's only ten in the morn," the butler stammered. "Yes, Your Grace," he amended beneath the commanding stare despite the realization that the countess hadn't yet risen.

"Mrs. Brunner," Grimes halted the head housekeeper outside the breakfast room. "Have Niles wake Countess Tember at once. Lord Hargrove has arrived. Tell her I'll have the young ladies go to him at once."

"Lord Hargrove!" A meaningful smile wreathed Mrs. Brunner's face. Countess Tember's ambitions were well known below stairs.

"At once," Grimes told her, then entered the breakfast room.

"My lady, Miss Louisa," the butler paused, momentarily

49

taken aback by the grim-faced pair. "The duke of Hargrove and Mr. Medlock await in the Oriental Salon."

Lady Margaret blanched.

Squelching her own fear, Louisa asked, "Is Grandmama dressed?"

"Mrs. Brunner is seeing to that now."

"I had so hoped he wouldn't come," Lady Margaret sniffed.

Grimes looked to Miss Elliott for further instruction.

"We'll join the gentlemen at once," Louisa assured him. She took Meg's arm as they left the breakfast room.

"Since his grace has brought Francis he can't mean any harm. Come, we'd best be with them when Grandmama comes down. How thoughtless of him to come so early."

"Don't speak too harshly, Louisa," Lady Margaret reproved as she wrung her hands. "What can it mean?"

"Perhaps he wishes to make sure of my punishment?"

"Why would he have brought Fran—Mr. Medlock?"

An odd look flicked across Louisa's features. "He wishes to rescue him from a horrid fate—marriage to me," she said darkly, then laughed. "Perhaps he'll do me a service. Grandmama wouldn't dare contradict him if he prohibited the marriage."

"Louisa, have you no feelings? Poor Mr. Medlock." Concern and dismay filled Lady Margaret's eyes. "He would be disheartened if such a thing happened. He speaks highly of you."

The impossibility of these words evoked a chortle of laughter from Louisa as the young ladies entered the salon.

"Lady Margaret, charmingly beautiful," Hargrove said, sauntering toward them. "And Miss Elliott. How good to see you in such high spirits this morn." He searched her features but found no clue to her feelings.

"Thank you, Your Grace," Louisa said, sinking into a curtsy and lowering her gaze at the sudden confusion at seeing him aroused. When she straightened a mocking respect was in place on his features.

"Mr. Medlock," Lady Margaret greeted the obviously distressed young gentleman with a warm smile.

"Dear Lady—Hamilton. A good—a good morn to you," Francis stuttered, twisting a gold fob. "Told Lord Hargrove it was too early," he said, daring to meet her gaze.

"Louisa and I are early risers, Mr. Medlock. It's no inconvenience," Meg assured him. She turned to Hargrove and Louisa and found them silently gazing at one another.

"Will you be seated, Your Grace? The countess shall join us shortly."

"Your Grace," she repeated when neither moved.

Hargrove looked at her blankly.

With a nervous smile, Lady Margaret motioned to the sofa and settee near the fireplace. "Shall we be seated?"

Hargrove mentally shook himself. "Of course," he said, moving to allow Louisa to pass.

After several moments Francis broke the silence. "It's a fine morning." Lady Margaret's smile caused him to forget what he intended to say next. "A bloody fine one," he repeated.

"Fine indeed." Hargrove cursed his sudden lack of wits. "May is noted for such mornings."

Struck by the absurdity, Louisa said, "Indeed, Your Grace?"

Hargrove stiffened.

"His grace—Lord Hargrove," Francis motioned awkwardly at the duke, "his grace thought we might go on an outing this morn."

"A picnic to be specific," Hargrove said stiffly. "My cook has assured me of a feast."

"And if we have other plans?" Louisa asked contrarily.

Lady Margaret and Francis straightened, exchanged fear-filled glances.

"But we do not—" both stated quickly.

Countess Tember flowed into the salon. "Your Grace, you young men are quite impetuous." She blessed them with a pleased smile. "But accountably so." Taking a seat beside Lady Margaret, Countess Tember beamed expectantly at Hargrove.

"I trust it's not an incommodious time, my lady," Hargrove said smoothly despite his inner turmoil.

"How could it be?" she trilled her protest.

"Medlock and I were hoping to gain permission to take your granddaughters on a picnic this morn."

"That would be delightful," the countess preened happily. "That is one of Lady Margaret's favorite things." She took hold of her granddaughter's hand. "And most considerate of you to include Louisa after last eve."

"The four of us shall be seeing a great deal of one another," Hargrove cut her off. "If you've no objection."

"Objection? Your Grace," Countess Tember protested. "It's my fondest wish—and yours, isn't it?" She squeezed Lady Margaret's hand.

Meg nodded, her eyes downcast.

A sense of betrayal welled within Louisa. *He'll force Meg.*

Countess Tember's voice sharpened. "Louisa."

"Yes, Grandmama?"

"Go with Lady Margaret and change your gown. Wait," she halted her at the door. "Your curtsy," the old woman demanded.

"There's no need," Hargrove said firmly. "I forego the practice—among family." He tried unsuccessfully to catch Louisa's eye.

"Go on then child," Countess Tember irritably waved dismissal.

* * *

"We best hurry," Meg told Louisa when she stopped by her room a few moments later.

"I don't want to go on a picnic with 'his grace,' " Louisa said with a stamp of her foot. "And why must I wear this gown? Pale colors become you, Meg."

"You'll be with Mr. Medlock and you're wearing that gown because it pleases Grandmama who dislikes seeing you in bright colors.

"And you're to be grateful to Lord Hargrove," Lady Margaret continued. "He's doing you a vast service in being seen with you this morn. Many heard of the incident last eve," she said, trying to fasten the gown's buttons for her fidgeting cousin.

"You're praising him?"

"He's kind. Grandmama as much as said last eve that you were to wed Mr. Medlock before the month was out. The duke's insisting you accompany us will forestall that."

Unexplainable dismay filled Louisa. "I didn't ask it of him."

"It's no matter. Hurry. You know how Grandmama upsets Mr. Medlock."

Filled with gratitude, Lady Margaret chatted amiably with the duke while Louisa and Francis grew steadily more silent. All efforts to draw them out proved futile. Awkwardness descended upon the party.

Louisa's behavior confounded Hargrove. She showed no interest in Medlock but exhibited a profound dislike of him. *Why did she let me hold her*? he mused silently. *Did I imagine her response*?

Meg paused as she made to step down from the landau after they reached the park. "Is something troubling you, Your Grace?"

"When I'm with someone as charming as you, my lady?" he returned light-heartedly and lifted her lightly to the ground. "You're very beautiful."

His smiling approval knit a knot of fear about Meg's heart but she gave a curtsy and took his arm.

On the path a short distance away, Francis and Louisa awaited the pair. "How'll we manage a picnic?" Louisa asked when no basket or bundle of food was removed from the carriage.

"It's arranged," Hargrove answered. "I thought we'd enjoy a stroll first. The Mall is well-shaded," he said motioning to the broad tree-lined avenue that stretched from Buckingham House to the Admiralty.

Meg glanced at close-by St. James Palace, running parallel to the mall and at the *ton*, society's elite, which strolled near it and surmised Hargrove's reasoning. She smiled her gratitude. "A walk would be just the thing."

Hargrove bowed and handed her to Medlock. "We shall follow," he told Francis and offered a stunned Louisa his arm.

Watching Hargrove while Meg and Francis strolled away, Louisa experienced a rush of conflicting emotions. The urge to discover the reason for this public show of favor proved strongest.

"Shall we?" he asked, beginning to feel idiotic holding his arm out.

"Why?"

Hargrove lowered his arm, studying her curiously.

She attempted a glare of her grandmother's hauteur. "There's no need for this display of approval."

"But there is," he assured her.

Louisa watched his eyes darken to deep sea blue and her heart leapt. A surge of warmth coursed through her beneath his tender gaze and raised a desire she couldn't deny. "Why?" she half-whispered.

A sudden fear hit him. "Lady Margaret entreated me."

"She did?" Her gaze swung to her delicate cousin strolling so happily beside Francis. "She did?" Louisa repeated, indignation creeping into her words.

Cursing this wretched handling of the matter, Hargrove answered, "I couldn't refuse her."

Their gaze held for a long, mutually searching moment.

"No, of course not." Louisa took his arm. "Are you doing this because you have—have a fondness for Meg?"

An odd smile played about Hargrove's lips. "Why is my fondness or lack of it for Lady Margaret of interest to you?"

Though his tone was teasing Louisa shied from the question. "What's your reason for inviting Mr. Medlock and me?"

Hargrove laid a hand atop Louisa's.

Blushing, she tried to pull hers free. "Will you answer me?" she asked, her heart thundering in her ears.

"No, Miss Elliott," Hargrove said with regret. "We aren't here to add to last eve's disaster."

A spark of anger flared. "You needn't fear for my reputation, Your Grace."

"Listen my dear little scapegrace," Hargrove said, his grip tightening, "you're not going to make a scene."

"Why shouldn't I? So Meg won't be upset?"

"For Zeus' sake," exploded Hargrove in an undertone. "Must you be so single-minded?" His eye caught sight of a landau and a languid flutter of lace. "Smile," he commanded crisply. "That's Brummel's phaeton. The *beau monde* hangs on his every word. He shall tell everyone—"

Louisa didn't realize his words went unfinished after Hargrove noticed her paleness. She hurried her steps to rejoin the other two and he didn't delay.

"Take this direction," Hargrove motioned to Francis and then positioned himself between Louisa and Meg.

Meg laughed delightedly. "What's this?" The sight of an elegantly uniformed footman arranging a cloth-draped table with crystal and cutlery beneath the cool canopy of a large tree on the green of St. James amazed her. "I've never seen a picnic of this kind," she beamed up at Hargrove.

"It's magnificent," Francis agreed with a sad sigh.

Hargrove gave Louisa a faint smile. "I hope it pleases."

"This is by your order," she blurted.

"Hush," Francis glowered.

Reading the signs of temper upon Louisa's features, Meg said, "I'm famished. Can we eat?"

"Of course, my lady." Hargrove offered her his arm.

Francis whispered urgently, "Louisa."

Realizing she had upset both of them, Louisa forced a smile. "Please assist me, Francis. It's comforting to have the aid of a *gentleman*," she said pointedly.

The picnic passed with conversation maneuvered away from conflict by Lady Margaret. Mutual baiting between Hargrove and Louisa entertained them but worried the other two.

Louisa's satisfaction at equaling Lord Hargrove's sparring wit evaporated when she accidentally knocked over her wine glass. Immediately a footman was at her elbow, daubing up the red stain. "It's all right," she assured the man.

"Let me refill your glass, miss," he urged.

"If you must." A sudden recognition came. "Aren't you Collins? Didn't Lady Landley dismiss you last eve?"

"You may go," Hargrove dismissed the footman, his look quelling any response.

Louisa flared at his interference but said nothing. A few moments later she rose. "Please excuse me, Meg. Francis. Your grace. I wish to stroll after such a repast."

Medlock reluctantly made to rise. "I'll come with you."

"No," she said firmly, "continue your discussion."

Her tone and the glint in her eye defied dispute. Francis sank back into his seat. "As you wish."

"Don't you think someone should go with Miss Elliott? Perhaps one of my footmen?" Hargrove suggested.

"No, Your Grace," Lady Margaret said with a pale imitation of a smile. "It's best to let Louisa to do as she wishes."

"Yes, Your Grace," Francis added knowledgeably.

A footman coughed apologetically beside Hargrove. "From that gentleman." He indicated a short, dark man and held out a salver with a folded page upon it.

Hargrove picked up the paper and unfolded it. After a brief glance he thrust it into his pocket. "Please excuse me."

"Of course," Lady Margaret assured him. Watching him saunter away she relaxed for the first time that morn.

"I told you never to come to me in public," Lord Hargrove rebuked guiding the man to a hedge beyond sight of his guests.

"Excusez-moi, il est très important." He wrung his hands and continued in heavily accented English. "The gentleman does not wish comply. Indeed, he speaks of going to M. Castlereagh."

"Calm yourself. He can't harm you. No, it must be a ploy to pay less. You told him I'd have the plans in a week?"

"Oui."

"Meet me at the usual place this eve. Go now," Hargrove ordered curtly and strode back toward his guests.

On the other side of the hedge Louisa's heart pounded. *What can it mean? Of whom are they speaking?* A lump filled her throat. Castlereagh was head of the War Department.

Plans in a week. Pay less. Hargrove a traitor?

Impossible, her heart chimed.

Walking forward, she saw Lord Hargrove and Lady Margaret, their laughter softly echoing. "Oh, Meg," Louisa whispered, "what am I to do?"

Chapter Seven

"It's warm this eve," Lady Margaret commented to Louisa as she checked her appearance in the rooms set aside for the ladies' convenience at the Lambert's soiree. "Such a crush," she mused.

"I'll stay here for a time, Meg." Louisa sat dejectedly on a Chippendale chair that had seen better days.

"Don't be silly. Mr. Medlock is waiting. And Grandmama shall be watching," Meg said with forced gaiety.

"Francis and I merely trample upon each others feet," she grimaced. "Go on. His grace may have arrived."

A troubled cast flickered across Lady Margaret's features.

"Do you care for him, Meg? I mean, he's called and taken us driving or riding every day since the picnic. Each night he appears wherever we go. Has he said anything?"

"What can he have said to me that you do not know?" she laughed. "We're never alone despite Grandmama's efforts."

Louisa bit her lip. "If you wish I'll speak to Francis and plead a headache on the morrow."

"Oh, no, Louisa. You mustn't," Lady Margaret sank to her knees before her. "His grace is a gentleman but—"

"You're always smiling and laughing with him—"

"I'm being polite." Meg blinked back tears. "Might he believe I'm encouraging him?"

"But you seem so happy when we are all—"

Shaking her head, Meg rose and returned to the mirror. "Lord Hargrove is handsome, kind, everything a woman could want in a husband. I'm the most wretched girl," she sniffed.

Louisa rose and gently turned her cousin to face her. "Are you going to allow Grandmama to force you to the match?"

"You can't understand, Louisa. It's always been easy for you to stand against Grandmama. I've never even dared to try.

"Aunt Edwina assures me happiness will come later when there are children."

"Meg, don't fool yourself. Cousin Portia is wretched."

"Then why haven't you refused Francis?" Meg said with cold desperation. "You see. It'll always be as Grandmama dictates." Meg moved to the door then paused.

"I'll come in a moment," Louisa told her. She moved to a settee and moved a screen to shield it from the door.

Lady Margaret hesitated until she was behind the screen.

"It's so, I tell you," a high-pitched voice reached Louisa's ears as she lay on the settee. "They say Hargrove is hard put these days."

"But he carries on in the same style," another objected.

"They all do until the moment the duns send them to the Marshallsea," the first said knowledgeably. "Though it'd be a shame to see Lord Hargrove in debtors prison."

"I can't believe it."

"Haven't you seen the way he is dangling after the Hamilton chit? Even tolerates that goose of a cousin. The countess of Tember is eager for the match. I've heard that Hamilton Manor is part of the dowry luring him."

"No!"

"Yes, and marriage to a beauty with money is far more appealing than some of the other means of restoring the family wealth that are being whispered about."

"Other ways?" the second giggled.

"I'm not one to gossip, but Napoleon pays highly for—"

Straining forward to hear what was being said as they left, Louisa tumbled from the settee. She rushed to the door but saw no one near. Hargrove's proud image rose vividly in her mind. Conceited. Arrogant. Disconcerting. She sighed.

But a traitor? Her heart balked. *And what of Meg?* she thought. *What if it proves true?* "The marriage must be prevented," she said. "Proof," *I must get it.*

Back in the salon she found her resolve challenged by Hargrove's magnificent figure momentarily framed in the elaborate gilt entrance.

"I thought you'd never return," Lady Margaret greeted her. "Why, what's wrong, Louisa? How pale you are."

"I'm fine." Louisa's gaze remained on the tall figure. *Don't think of the price to him*, she told herself, denying there would be any to her own heart.

"My lady," Lord Hargrove bowed to Meg. "Miss Elliott."

"I must find Francis," she blurted and hurried away.

"Now what've I done?" Hargrove inquired with a heavy sigh. "The way Miss Elliott looked at me one would think I was a traitor."

"Hardly, Your Grace." Lady Margaret smiled despite herself. "Louisa has the headache. At least I hope it's nothing worse." Her gaze followed her cousin, concern wrinkled her brow. "She's not been herself this week past."

Hargrove smiled wryly. "Has that been a relief?"

"No, Your Grace. Surely you've noticed how quiet she has become?" Lady Margaret protested.

"Perhaps she's tired of the social whirl?" he offered.

"You truly don't know Louisa," Lady Margaret laughed. "It's I who am weary of it."

"Lord Hargrove, so good to see you," Lady Lambert purred. "I see you've found Lady Margaret," she simpered behind her fan. "The orchestra is about to play. Do enjoy yourself." Giving a knowing smile she flitted away.

Meg sighed.

Hargrove offered his arm. "Shall we?"

"It's the longest eve I've ever had," Louisa complained to Francis who had brought her an ice.

"We could—could dance again," he offered apologetically.

"Not I." She sipped the cooling drink. "You could ask Grandmama if we may leave early," Louisa said hopefully.

Francis looked at her in dismay. "But we've been here only an hour. Guests are still arriving." He pointed to Viscount Brice who had paused inside the salon.

They watched him approach the duke.

"Why's Lord Hargrove excusing himself?" she thought aloud.

Francis shrugged disinterestedly. "Perhaps Lord Brice brought a message."

Suspicion flared anew when Hargrove left. "Come, Francis," Louisa pulled the hapless gentleman after her as she went in pursuit of the duke.

"Louisa, where are you going?" Meg asked as they passed.

"I'll explain later. Stay here with Grandmama. Hurry, Francis." She tossed him an impatient frown. Releasing his hand, she pressed through the crush without him.

Outside Louisa heard Hargrove order, "The Shepherd's Inn beyond Houndslow Heath." Her eyes lit with inspiration.

"Come, Francis," she greeted him. "We must follow him."

He daubed his perspiration-beaded brow. "Follow whom?"

"My cloak, please," Louisa ordered a footman.

"Come back inside," Francis protested.

"Thank you," she told the footman as she took her cloak. Taking Francis' hand, she waved down a hackney.

"What do you mean to do?"

"You must come," Louisa pleaded. "I'll explain as we travel. It wouldn't please Grandmama if you let me go alone." Sensing victory she ordered, "Shepherd's Inn," and clambered into the coach before Medlock could forestall her.

Sighing heavily, Francis followed, his fear of the countess's wrath overcoming his dread of the scrape she was surely leading him into.

"We're following Lord Hargrove," Louisa explained when they were safely underway. "I must get proof."

"Proof?" Francis asked, astonished at following a duke.

"You'll find this difficult to believe, even as I do—did. Hargrove is a—a traitor."

Francis let loose an amused bark. "It's a poor jest."

"I overheard Hargrove speaking to a Frenchman the day of the picnic. This evening I heard that he is in distressed circumstances. Then Lord Brice appears and he takes a hackney to an out of the way inn," she finished in a rush.

"Which proves nothing."

"The French landed in Wales in '97 and Lord Brice is Welsh. Haven't there been rumors that the Welsh support France?" she asked. "Surely you've heard about Lord Hargrove's financial difficulties?"

He squirmed uncomfortably. "There—there's been some rumors. But one can't believe gossip."

"We'll have proof this eve that it's not innuendo," Louisa stated with false confidence.

Francis's stomach lurched at the disaster he saw forming.

"We'll follow Lord Hargrove into the Shepherd's Inn—"

"You've no plan," Francis said with vast relief. "We can't learn anything." He made to halt the driver.

"No," Louisa stopped him. "I don't know exactly how, but we'll discover what Lord Hargrove is about."

Francis wrung his hands. "Oh, dear."

"Be quiet," Louisa said sharply, her own nerves taut. "You can wait in the hackney," she offered apologetically.

Apprehension and uncertainty gripped Louisa when she finally stood outside the inn's door.

"Let's go back," Francis pleaded behind her.

Gathering courage, Louisa forced her hand to the door and strode in. Smoke and a strong sweaty odor greeted her. Loud laughter and rough talk filled the large ale room to one side; an equally boisterous group was clustered around the tables in the opposite room. Her eyes swept over the men, then to the corridor before her and the stairs at the far end.

"Whatcha be needin', me pretty?" A large-bellied man, his front teeth missing, and four huge mugs clasped in each hand stood before her.

"Why—why, a chamber," she stammered. "Two in fact," she added, remembering Francis.

"What's yer mum got ta say about yer being here," he surveyed her shrewdly, winked at Francis.

"It's not as you think," Francis said, reddening.

"That's naught to me," the fat man laughed. "Not likely any'll question me about yer doin's."

"What on earth—" exclaimed Francis when Louisa put her arms about his neck.

"Quiet," she whispered. "He is going up the stairs."

"She's a bit nervous," Francis stuttered to the leering innkeeper. "The rooms if you please," he gulped.

"Take any that be empty," the man laughed. "And five schillings afore you pass."

"Yes, of course." Francis frantically searched his money pouch with trembling fingers. "If the countess learns of this," he muttered as he handed over the coins.

Louisa dragged him into the corridor.

Francis wiped the perspiration from his brow. "What if his grace sees us? Let's leave," he begged.

Louisa prodded him forward. "Listen at that door."

At the end of the corridor the pair halted, unsuccessful in discovering Hargrove.

"Can we go now?" Francis asked hopefully. Hearing Hargrove's voice he grabbed Louisa's arm, but was too late.

Both of them tried to dash away, but collided in a heap on the floor. Struggling upright amid a tangle of cloak, skirts, and petticoats Louisa heard Hargrove's deep laugh.

"An eager pair," someone jested and the door closed again.

Finally unraveling themselves, the pair dashed for the stairs when they heard Hargrove again. A wild glance assured Louisa he hadn't seen them but the laughter of those they passed sent her hurtling down the stairs and out the door. Francis nearly ran over her in the rush to enter the waiting hackney.

"I bloody well thought the end had come," Francis swore. He tugged his cravat and vest into a semblance of order. "Would never have been able to explain. He might even have called me out. What would the countess have said to that?"

"We shouldn't have lost our wits," Louisa admonished.

The hackney lurched, throwing her into Francis's arms. "Do slow the driver," she scolded pushing away. "He's bent on perdition."

"What's he to think, the way we hurtled out," Francis retorted. "It's your doing." He tapped the roof.

"Slow down. Take us to Number 45 Hanover Square." He shook his head. "How am I to explain this to the countess?

A common inn." Anger emboldened him. "It was madness. No one would go there but for an assignation."

"Assignation?" Louisa was glad for the darkness shielding her flaming cheeks. "You don't mean he met—that he—"

"It's far more likely than your wild tale," Francis answered petulantly. "It's done by all men of the *ton*." Realizing what he had said, he squirmed.

"I mean, well—it's not a proper subject." He folded his arms and clamped his lips together.

Gossip, rumors, observation had imparted such intelligence to Louisa. Yet she was shocked and in a sense, betrayed. It was far easier to accept Hargrove as a traitor. She gulped down the lump in her throat. *It's another reason to save Meg from him*, she thought as she brushed away a tear.

Chapter Eight

"Stop this chatter." Countess Tember's cold voice quieted her sisters and cousins seated in the Oriental Salon. "You speak as if the matches were accomplished. They aren't."

Smiles faded. The ladies shifted uneasily.

"But his grace has been driving with Lady Margaret every day," Cousin Mary began.

"And dances with her each night," Cousin Jane nodded.

"You should be happy with this progress," Lady Lindley said fingering her gold pendant. "Many say—"

"What worth are others' words? Two years past Hargrove squired Lorraine Fawnsworth about for a month. Is she now his duchess?" The countess slammed her hand on the chair's arm.

"At least young Medlock has taken the bridle well," Cousin Jane said pursing her lips primly.

"Even there, we have no announcement published in the *Gazette*," Countess Tember blustered angrily.

"Surely, Francis needs but a gentle nudge," Lady Elizabeth protested weakly. "Mary saw them leave the soiree

early last eve." Her head bobbed accusingly at the countess.
"Alone."

"Louisa had the headache," Lady Edwina said in defense.

An upraised hand silenced all. "The child has been reprimanded for such improper behavior and confined to her
chamber. But it's more her chaperone's failing." The cold
rebuke bowed her daughter's head.

"I had hoped that a week hence, on the eve of the
Devonshire ball that an announcement could be made."

"But for which?" Lady Elizabeth asked.

"Truly, Elizabeth," Countess Tember snorted, "Margaret,
of course. But haven't you heard the rumors concerning
Lord Hargrove? I'll not be taken for the fool, even by a duke.
Medlock's declaration must be postponed. I'll not have Lady
Margaret embarrassed by Louisa's marriage if her own does
not come to pass.

"We must provide closer chaperonage for Margaret," the
countess continued. "While we don't want to endanger her
prospects, we must be cautious."

Countess Tember snapped her fingers. "One of us is to be
near Lady Margaret at all times when Lord Hargrove is
near."

"All this after you wanted us to maneuver them into a situation where they'd be found alone," Lady Lindley groused.

"You've forgotten the gossip. If it proves true we must
extricate Margaret with no damage to her reputation."

"Do you really believe the tales about Lord Hargrove's
business failings?" asked Cousin Jane.

"I mean to take his uncle to task at the appointment he set
with me two days hence. He means to talk over the dowry
but I'll have none of that without assurances," the countess
said.

The tinkling clatter of falling metal outside the salon's
closed doors startled the women.

"See what that is," Countess Tember demanded.

Outside in the corridor, Louisa frantically tried to re-attach the iron gauntlet to the miniature suit of armor she had backed into when she retreated from listening at the door.

Coming out, Lady Edwina surmised the circumstance at once. "Go to your room," she whispered fiercely, taking the gauntlet.

Louisa took her muslin skirts in hand and dashed around the corner just as the door opened.

"What on earth? Edwina, what are you about?" Jane snorted.

"I—I passed too close and—"

"As if this suit of armor hasn't been here these past thirty years," Jane said, shaking her head. "Do come back in; we are just finishing."

Lady Margaret followed Louisa's hurried entrance into her bedchamber. "Did Grandmama discover you?"

"Just Aunt Edwina," her cousin said between gasps. "We can both be saved—from the matches." She clasped Meg's hands.

"Not that nonsense again," Lady Margaret said sadly.

"No. I heard Grandmama say that if your match fails then mine will also be set aside," she said happily.

"But *mine* will not be," Meg said with downcast eyes.

"You don't know what I've learned. All we have to do is find proof."

"Proof?" Puzzlement filled Lady Margaret, then misgiving at Louisa's determined expression.

"Lord Hargrove is having financial difficulties. To recoup his losses he is—well, he's trying to make a match with you. And he has—has agreed to sell government documents to the French.

"Francis and I almost caught him last eve but—" Her exuberance lessened at the memory. "We only have to watch him—"

"Louisa, stop this flummery," Meg said angrily. "It's enough that you speak so lightly of Francis," she paced agitatedly, "and make him endure your flighty hoyendish ways. Now you malign his grace. Lord Hargrove has done naught but strive to please you and—" Tears spilled down pale cheeks. Sobbing, Lady Margaret fell into her cousin's arms.

After calming her Louisa asked gently, "What is it, Meg?"

"Is there any chance that Grandmama will not make me marry him?" she asked tremulously.

"If we could find proof that he is a spy," Louisa answered. A deep sadness filled her. She pushed it aside. "With your help I am certain it can be done."

"My—my help? But I couldn't," Lady Margaret protested.

"Then we'll both be lost," Louisa told her.

"What do you have in mind?" Meg asked. She smiled weakly at her cousin's surprise. "Do you have a plan?"

"Well, on the morrow Grandmama will be occupied by a visit from the duke's uncle. We can rise early, leave the house and hire a hackney. We'll take up watch at Lord Hargrove's home and follow him when he leaves."

"What can that prove?"

"We must try it." Louisa paused reflectively. "I could ask Francis to take us though he may not be easy to persuade."

"Why? Did something happen after the soiree?"

"We followed Lord Hargrove but lost him," Louisa lied, knowing her cousin's reaction if she should learn the truth.

"That's all?"

"Yes, and that's the worst that can happen to us. Please

say you will, Meg?" Louisa pleaded. Reading her cousin's capitulation she felt no victory, but refused to acknowledge why.

Lord Hargrove grimaced at Lord Brice's laughter. "It'd not be so amusing if it were you instead of me."

"It's too humorous, Keane. I can visualize it. Your ducal hauteur, shocked to discover two ladies following you. Did you truly take them through Billingsgate?" He chuckled anew.

"And down St. James in the afternoon," Hargrove said grimly.

Brice raised an eyebrow calculatingly. "That was a bit harsh. No lady appears there at that time of day."

"No less than she deserved," he answered curtly. "I dragged her through every market, every narrow alley I could find before I led them back to their door."

"What I'd have given to have seen Miss Elliott's face, heard her words when you opened the hackney's door and offered to help her down."

"Only Lady Margaret's presence saved her from the set down I had planned. How she ever persuaded that fragile beauty to take part in the escapade is beyond me." Hargrove's anger was fed by his chagrin upon discovering the beauty cowering within when he had expected to find only Louisa. "I thought the Hamilton chit was going to faint."

"But you gallantly eased all her fears, assured her how commodious it was for you both to have arrived at the same moment." Lord Brice's unfailing accuracy irked Hargrove.

"Was there any other way open to me? Give me just five minutes with that incorrigible miss," he swore. "I will give her the lesson of her life."

"Quite possibly."

"Damnation, Glynn, what am I to do?" Lord Hargrove surged to his feet and paced restlessly.

Lord Brice tightly pressed his lips, lest he laugh outright. "Did you learn why you were followed?"

"It's a bloody puzzle." Hargrove's scowl deepened. "And at a time when I need no further complications. I must remove to Hargrove Retreat soon if the Badden matter is to be successfully concluded."

"It goes well?"

"Well enough—that woman is avaricious."

"Word of your financial difficulties has spread rapidly."

"It must be believed."

"There are those who refuse to give credence to the non-sense. You've always had that upright, starched aura of respectfulness." The viscount smiled at his friend's frown.

"I've heard it whispered that you are dangling after the Hamilton girl for her dowry."

"Thunderation!" Hargrove swore.

"It's a logical if unexpected, conclusion."

"No wonder she holds me in such disdain."

"When you return from Hargrove Retreat you may explain all to Lady Margaret," Lord Brice baited. He rose lithely. "Will you be gone from London overlong?"

Hargrove grimaced at his friend. "Perhaps it's for the best," he said after a long pause. "It'll give me a chance to clear my thoughts after this other bloody business is done. What a foul taste it brings."

"Necessity isn't often pleasant. It's easier done if not dwelt upon," advised the viscount. "Many are endangered if you don't discover who's responsible for the information leak. If you can entice Lady Badden to expose herself—"

"Let's speak of pleasanter matters." Hargrove sat and

absently motioned his friend to do likewise. Louisa came unbidden to mind. *What a maddening dance she will lead some unfortunate chap,* he thought, *but Medlock won't be the one.*

Chapter Nine

"Isn't it curious that Lady Lindley has become our shadow?" Hargrove smiled at Lady Margaret as they stood in the elaborately decorated Devonshire ballroom amidst an elegant crush.

"I hadn't noticed, Your Grace," Meg murmured. All eve she had been tremblingly awaiting Louisa's demand that she assist in some outrageous scheme.

"My uncle called on your grandmother during the week."

A blush rose to Lady Margaret's fair cheeks, dismay wrinkled her brow. "I know."

"I regret that it doesn't please you," he said, taking perverse displeasure that any lady wouldn't be flattered by consideration as his bride.

"Of—of course it didn't displease me," Meg stammered, and looked wildly around for some escape.

"Lord Spenser, how good to see you this eve," Hargrove greeted the passing gentleman.

The marquess bowed over Lady Margaret's hand. "Lovely, my dear."

"How kind of you, my lord," she said smiling shyly.

"What of the new proposal before Parliament, my lady? A roasting it has received in the pamphlets, eh?" Lord Spenser nudged Hargrove with a knowing grin.

"I am—am unaware—"

"Oh, come, come, my dear. Any wife of Hargrove will have to keep abreast of such matters. Ah, I see Fox has finally arrived. Must speak with him. My lady, Your Grace," he bowed and left them.

"Hargrove," Lord Avanley said as he strolled up to the pair. "Introduce me to this lovely lady," the young lord said with a mischievous wink.

When the greetings were complete Avanley remarked, "Haven't seen you of late, Your Grace." He smiled good-naturedly. "Now I see why." He bowed to a blushing Lady Margaret. "Do you also share Hargrove's enthusiasm for Wilberforce's anti-slavery, my lady?" he asked archly.

"I believe he has some good points," Meg said vaguely and began to turn the conversation just as the duke of Devonshire joined the small group with a curt nod.

"I thought that damned receiving line would never end," he told Hargrove. "We must meet with Bessborough and North this eve. Touchy matter, this missing document business."

Lady Margaret's gaze flashed to Hargrove. The flicker of distaste that crossed his features was more convincing than any argument Louisa had offered. Glancing across the crowded ballroom she saw with relief that Louisa and Francis approached.

"We must discuss this matter privately," Devonshire said as they neared and exchanged greetings.

"This is an evening for enjoyment," he told Avanley. "Perhaps later."

"Does Your Grace bother with politics?" Louisa asked with a touch of sarcasm, ignoring Francis' death grip on her arm.

"Miss Elliott, you do Hargrove an injustice," Lord Avanley laughed. "Didn't you read in the *Gazette* that—"

"Many pay for their own puffs, my lord." She smiled sweetly at the baron. "Even Charles Fox—"

"Excuse us," Francis said with a strained voice. He forced Louisa to walk away with him. "Countess Tember awaits us," he threw back before the startled miss on his arm could object.

Lord Devonshire's sharp bark of laughter followed them. "For a moment I thought we had a young chit who could speak with some intelligence on the issues of the day."

"But she can," Meg said without thinking. "Louisa reads all the reports published on parliament and the political pamphlets. It's a great interest of hers," she defended.

"And one of yours, of course," her host smiled placatingly.

"Actually no," Meg continued with unusual boldness despite the rapid pounding of her heart. "I find it tiresome and far too complicated."

"Well said," Lord Avanley bowed to her with a flourish. "Bluestockings aren't to my taste," he winked. "Your Grace, will you surrender Lady Margaret to me for the minuet?"

"Certainly."

He offered his arm. "May I?"

Lady Margaret took it instantly. Her relief in leaving Hargrove's side quavered when she met Lady Landley's frown. Ignoring it she smiled at Avanley and launched into a discussion of Handel's latest offering with seasoned aplomb.

"An odd choice for you, that one," Lord Devonshire glanced sharply at Hargrove. "But so was mine." His smile lapsed. "Rumors have spread."

"Which ones?" he asked, arching a brow.

"It's terribly warm." Louisa fanned her face with sudden enthusiasm as she saw Lord Hargrove leave the ballroom through one of the doors opening onto the Devonshire gardens. "Such a crush," she smiled wanly at Francis. "I'll step out on the veranda for a few moments. No, you needn't accompany me," she stayed him. "I'll remain close to the doors.

"See, Grandmama is stepping out. I'll be safe with her."

"Yes, bloody good," Francis said with a solemn nod, his eyes already searching out another figure in the magnificent ballroom.

"You needn't worry if I don't return immediately," Louisa told him, heedless of his inattention in her rush to keep Hargrove in sight. Carefully avoiding Countess Tember, she edged away from the lantern-lit veranda. When safely in the shadows Louisa began wandering down the paths in search of the duke. A burst of giggles from an arbor froze her steps.

A nearby rustling prompted her to move forward. She glanced about nervously. *I shouldn't have ventured so far.* The darkness enveloped her and she turned back, cautiously retreating. Louisa gasped when a man appeared before her.

He lurched forward and captured her with a drunken laugh.

The liquor-coated breath struck a cord of fear in Louisa. "Release me." She struggled to pull free.

"Zee lady weeshes, hic, some excitement, *non*," he laughed, trying to kiss her.

Revulsion and fear mixed as Louisa struggled. Suddenly an iron hand tore her from the man's hold and thrust her back. A tall, lithe shadow dealt him a solid facer. Her rescuer hurried her from the scene, halting in the protection of an arbor some distance away.

"Sir, I thank you." Louisa leaned against his steadying arm. A sense of familiarity rushed upon her. She wished the darkness not so deep as she strove to make out his features.

"Must you *always* be stumbling into trouble," Lord Hargrove said, his voice rough with concern.

"You." She backed away.

"What were you doing in that area of the gardens?" he demanded harshly. Hargrove took hold of her shoulders and gave her a shake.

"I was—was—merely walking." Louisa trembled.

"Didn't you realize the danger—" His anger died when Louisa trembled. A stronger more pervading emotion replaced it.

"No, you wouldn't have thought of it," Lord Hargrove muttered. He drew her forward despite the faint urging of his common sense. "It must have been frightening for you," he continued as his arms folded about her.

Louisa's mind swirled with the spike of excitement his nearness always prompted. A soft "Louisa" reached her ear, his breath caressed her neck. She laid her head against the softness of his fine lawn blouse, his masculine scent intensifying a bewildering rush of warmth.

His rapidly pulsing heartbeat matched her own. Drawing back slightly, she raised her eyes, searched his features in the flickering shadows. She raised her hand, touched his cheek.

"Louisa," he said in an agonized voice. His lips crushed hers.

All caution fled. With a soaring heart Louisa responded. Her ardor grew as everything but Lord Hargrove slipped into oblivion and an aching pleasure ruled.

Long moments later Countess Tember's voice pierced the silence and crashed the embracing couple back into reality.

"My God," Hargrove swore beneath his breath, his hold loosening. "What've I done?"

Louisa gasped in cold fear at his withdrawal which she sensed was more than physical. She raised a hand to her flaming face.

Hargrove reached for her but missed. "No, don't go."

"Is that you, Lord Hargrove?" Countess Tember halted his pursuit. "I must speak with you. Were you with someone just now?" she demanded when he reluctantly turned to face her.

"No." Hargrove's haughty tone ended further questions.

"Let's walk nearer the lighting, Your Grace," the countess said changing her tact. "One could fall here in the shadows."

"Yes, I know," he answered bitterly. Silently cursing his foolishness and the countess's appearance he offered his arm.

"You've been seeing my granddaughter, Lady Margaret, often these past weeks," Countess Tember continued, oblivious of his mood. "Many have noted. Just this eve Countess Levien asked me when the happy announcement would be made." She paused, aware of his sudden tenseness. "The Hargroves have always been honest and gentlemanly, Your Grace. I trust you'll not disappoint."

"I hope not, my lady," he answered curtly.

"Much damage would be done to an innocent if you withdraw without good reason," the countess continued ruthlessly.

"Lady Margaret'll not be harmed in any way by me, I assure you." Hargrove halted, removed her hand from his arm.

"Your word of honor, Your Grace?"

"You have it." An icy smile covered his bitterness.

"Oh, dear," Francis muttered, steeling himself at Louisa's approach, her agitation nerve-wrackingly visible. "We can't leave," he began before she halted.

Louisa waved her hand. "I must speak with you, Francis—privately." She took his arm and propelled him to one of the alcoves lining the ballroom.

"I don't think we should—" he tried to object.

"Be quiet and listen," she cut him off. Turning away she tried to compose herself. After a bit she asked, "What would you think—I mean, what would you think of a gentleman who is almost betrothed to one person and who—" she swallowed the lump in her throat, "who makes bold advances to her—her sister?"

"Advances?" Francis puzzled.

Louisa blushed fiercely. "Surely you know what I mean?"

Running a finger nervously between his collar and neck Francis blustered, "Of course."

"What should be done?"

"Why—he's a rake. He should be called out."

"Do you think the sister should tell—"

"No. Too insensitive," his voice trailed off. "Of whom are we speaking?"

"A friend—an acquaintance I chanced to see in the gardens. I can't say further," she lowered her eyes, her guilt at her response to Hargrove's kiss too well remembered.

"Of course," Francis agreed. "I'm happy not to know who the cad is. Would be deuced uncomfortable the next time I met him. You're quite right to remain silent," he assured her, hoping to guarantee it.

"But this has upset you. Let's find Lady Margaret. She'll restore your spirits." He took Louisa's arm and guided her from the alcove.

A rush of emotions bewildered Louisa momentarily when she saw Hargrove at her cousin's side. She hesitated but was propelled forward by an unyielding Francis.

"Miss Elliott," Hargrove nodded, his hopeful smile crushed by the accusing stare she presented. "I was just telling Lady Margaret that I must retire to Hargrove Retreat and am arranging a small party. I hope you'll accompany your cousin and the countess. And you too, Medlock."

"Delighted, Your Grace," Francis stammered.

"I'll expect you all." He bowed, and strolled away.

"Of all the brazen—" Louisa swallowed the remainder

when she noticed Meg's stare. "I'll not go," she ended weakly.

"Mr. Medlock, could you excuse us," Lady Margaret asked. "I must speak with Louisa."

With a nod, Francis walked away.

"Louisa, you were right about his grace," Meg said taking hold her hand. "This very eve the duke of Devonshire told him he must speak to him about missing papers, government papers. Louisa wasn't paying attention.

"What is it? What do you see?" Meg's gaze followed her cousin's.

"That footman is giving a message to Lord Hargrove. I must follow him. Make an excuse to Francis," she whispered and hurried away without giving Meg a chance to intervene.

"What now?" Francis asked quickly returning to Lady Margaret's side. "Oh, dear, forgive my tone, my lady. It's just that Louisa—"

"No offense taken, Mr. Medlock." She smiled wanly.

He watched Louisa's progress with baleful eyes. "I suppose I must follow."

"I suddenly feel faint, Mr. Medlock." Lady Margaret took hold of his arm. "Please walk me to the veranda."

"At once, my lady," Francis gently placed an arm about her. "It's far too warm this eve."

In the corridor Louisa hurriedly tiptoed forward. Seeing a footman she dashed behind a huge stuffed black bear. After he passed, she saw another man and Lord Hargrove pausing in the junction of two corridors. A third man, a large portfolio under his arm and a haggard look to his face, joined them.

"You may use his grace's study," the footman said, bowing deeply to the trio.

"You needn't show us the way, Ned," Hargrove told the lad then led the others inside.

Louisa waited until the footman had passed her then stepped from behind the bear. Assuming a haughty smile she called out to him. "My man," she commanded, "I was told there was someone to see me. Where's he?"

The startled footman turned to face her. "Madam, the last arrival was Mr. Green of the War Department and he wished to speak to Lord Hargrove. I fear someone has misinformed you."

Louisa snapped her fan open with convincing anger and swept past the footman. *War Department*, she thought. *Must I be right? I do not want to be right.*

Chapter Ten

Countess Tember hurried through the assortment of notes and invitations Grimes had brought to the morning room. "Still no word from Lord Hargrove," she said with a frown.

Lady Margaret looked up from her needlework. "But it's been a mere week."

"I daresay he doesn't wish to appear overanxious," Lady Edwina added.

"Yes, yes," the countess said, still frowning.

Louisa burst in the room. "Meg, it's as I feared." She halted at sight of her grandmother.

"Why must you persist in such unladylike behavior?" Countess Tember demanded irritably. "Walk, Louisa. Slowly at all times and never raise your voice."

"Yes, Grandmama," she said, moving the object in her hands belatedly behind her back.

The countess did not miss the guilty move. "What have you there?"

Louisa shrugged nonchalantly.

"You were in a rush to speak with Lady Margaret," her

grandmother prompted. "And possibly to show her what you hold behind your back."

"It is only the *Morning Chronicle*, Grandmama. There's an article on—" At her stern look, Louisa laid the paper in the countess's outstretched hand.

Countess Tember unfolded the paper. "Harrumph," she snorted. "Balderdash. Rubbish. No English peer is going to sell his government's secret documents to the French. What impudence the printers have these days.

"Come, Edwina. I wish to dictate a letter to Mr. Hunt. Then we'll see to packing for our journey. Everything must be perfect," she added after a slight pause and a pointed glance at Louisa. She rose and strode from the morning room, her daughter obediently hastening after her.

The moment they were gone Louisa scooped up the paper and plopped down beside her cousin. "See, Meg. I was right."

She scanned the print. "I don't see Lord Hargrove's name."

"Of course not, but it mentions a peer who has of late returned to his seat. Mr. Green brought Lord Hargrove the missing documents that night at Devonshire house and he's gone to his home at Colchester to hand them over to the enemy. I checked—it's near enough to the Channel."

"He'd never have invited guests if that were true," Lady Margaret protested.

"But it's the perfect disguise for what he's doing."

"I still don't think that we can—"

"If there were any other way, I'd take it," Louisa said with quiet passion.

"Are those tears?" Meg asked in surprise.

"I was only thinking we might be too late to stop him," Louisa said, rising and walking to the window.

"Too late? No, you can't mean to try—not in his own home?"

"We must. Last eve I was scarcely able to forestall a declaration from Francis." She turned, her hands tightly clenched, a grim cast to her features.

"Why do you not speak to him—to Mr. Medlock," Meg questioned softly.

"I know you think me fearless." Louisa sank to the floor before her. "But it isn't so. If I were to refuse him Grandmama would be furious. She'd banish me from you and I couldn't bear that." She took Meg's hand.

"I've been overset of late. Much as I dread the thought, if we fail, there'll be naught for me to do but wed Francis." A tear stole down her cheek and once again she tried to tell herself that the man who held her and kissed in Devonshire gardens was not worthy of Meg, or of her.

"Another glass of port, Medlock?" Lord Hargrove refilled the young man's glass without waiting for a reply. "Do be seated." He frowned. "I'm poor company this eve," he apologized, "but other guests shall be arriving on the morrow."

"Oh, dear. I did not mean to intrude too early."

"Nonsense," Hargrove assured him, hiding his irritation at the fawning gesture.

"I did offer to escort the countess and her party but she refused to have me." Medlock shrugged his acceptance of the rejection.

"No doubt," Hargrove hid his smile, "it's for the best. Women are not good travelers and can make even a short journey a wretched experience."

"And Louisa, Miss Elliott, is so—so unsteady of late," Francis ended and drank deeply.

"It's fortunate you did." Hargrove studied the young man closely. Medlock had improved in his opinion since his arrival at midday. During supper he had shown an intelligence and comprehension of political issues that till now had been concealed beneath shyness. *With a few more years*, Lord Hargrove thought, *he may well mature into material for parliament*.

"You and Miss Elliott are betrothed?"

"Yes. Well, no—not exactly. That is, there's an understanding between our families," Francis said wearily. "One doesn't easily avoid Countess Tember's—err, wishes."

Hargrove feigned nonchalance. "You don't wish the match?"

"I didn't mean to imply that. Louisa is—I am certain she must have several very amiable qualities," he stammered. "I wouldn't have Countess Tember believe I thought otherwise."

"Be assured the conversation is betwixt us alone," Hargrove assured him. "It's only that I thought Miss Elliott slightly difficult to direct."

"One does not direct Louisa. My, no. One prays she'll not spring forth with too bold a scheme. She has the uncanny ability to plunge one into the maddest plot before one realizes the danger," Francis said with a rush of feeling. "You simply wouldn't believe what she did the night of the Lambert soiree—" Medlock stumbled, realizing what he had almost betrayed.

"You'll find me most sympathetic," Lord Hargrove told him and filled their glasses again. "During my last days in London Miss Elliott had the effrontery to follow me about in a hackney.

"Would you have any idea why she'd do that?"

Francis gulped, ran a finger between his throat and the sudden choking tightness of his cravat. "Why, no."

Devilish delight curved his lips, then mild chagrin. "I'd never have led her on the wild chase through London had I realized Lady Margaret was with her."

"Lady—her ladyship?" burst from Francis, his color drained. "She involved Lady Margaret in—oh, it's beyond endurance." He surged to his feet. "That so gentle a creature, so fragile a lady—one of such tender sensibilities should be forced—" He halted, suddenly aware of Hargrove's intensely interested gaze.

"My apologies, Your Grace. I didn't mean to speak of your—of Lady Margaret so boldly," Francis said timidly. "If you'll excuse me, I'd like to retire."

"By all means," Hargrove said. A sympathetic smile lit his features as he bid his visitor a good eve.

"Show Mr. Medlock to his chamber," he commanded the footman outside the library. His heart soared as he returned to the library and refilled his glass. *So Medlock is in love with Lady Margaret.* The relief that flooded through him was short lived. *What about Louisa's heart?*

"Viscount Brice, Your Grace," his aged butler announced.

Lord Hargrove offered him a glass as the butler withdrew. "You're late, Glynn. What of Moler?"

"Safely ensconced in one of your chambers." Lord Brice accepted the glass; fatigue lined his features. "Some minor trouble hampered our arrival."

"Minor," Hargrove scoffed.

"Unfortunately the delay has raised a difficulty."

Hargrove grimaced guiltily. "Young Medlock's here. The Countess Tember and her party arrive on the morrow."

"What? But aren't the Baddens—"

"My cousin, Lady Thea and her husband, Lord Grenby, are also coming. They'll keep the Hamiltons entertained."

"You've gone mad, Keane," Glynn said wearily. "How can you hope to carry this off with such a mix?"

"The business can be done at the Crossed Arms in Colchester if necessary," Hargrove answered abruptly.

"Treason, seduction, and courtship? It should prove an interesting house party," Lord Brice noted softly.

"Let's hope it's successful—on all counts." Lord Hargrove raised his glass in challenging salute.

"Hargrove Retreat is truly marvelous. Is it true it was once a monastery?" Lady Angela Badden fawned over Lord Hargrove in the salon where all were to gather before supper.

"The first duke purchased it during the Disolution in the 16th century. This particular wing however, was added by my father," he said, trying to disengage without giving offense.

"It's so vast and the rooms so spacious." Her eyes ran greedily over the rococo ceiling. "Are there priest's holes?"

"Your own improvements are well done, Your Grace," Countess Tember reproved Lady Badden. "Your commodious improvements have not played havoc with the character of the house."

"Your estate does not lie far from here," the elderly Lord Badden ruminated aloud.

"The whole of the Hamilton estate marches alongside Hargrove land. Very auspicious, isn't it, Your Grace?" Lady Badden smirked pointedly as she moved to her husband's side.

"The Marquess of Grenby and Lady Grenby," the butler announced.

"Welcome Thea," Hargrove said warmly, vastly relieved. He embraced the petite, fiery-haired woman who was ten years his senior and then shook hands with her husband. "Sorry I wasn't able to greet you upon your arrival," he apologized, then brought the couple forward.

"My beautiful cousin shall be my hostess," he said smiling broadly at her. "I believe you are acquainted with most of my guests."

"Flattery won't ease the sharpness of my direction, Your Grace," Lady Thea laughed softly. "I was the only one to brave the ducal hauteur when he was in his younger days." She greeted the countess with a kiss.

"And you must be Lady Margaret," she smiled at the demure and pale young woman at Countess Tember's side. She acknowledged Meg's greeting and turned to Lady Edwina.

"How lovely you look this eve. May I join you?" She sat beside her. "We've much to reminisce about. Thank heaven's we were of the same age when I lived here." Lady Thea winked mischievously at Hargrove.

"Thea, may I present Miss Louisa Elliott, cousin to Lady Margaret, and Francis Medlock," Lord Hargrove introduced the pair standing to one side. "Lord and Lady Badden."

Lady Grenby arched a brow after acknowledging the introductions. "Is Glynn not here?"

"It warms a Welshman's cold heart to hear such words," the viscount said as he strode into the salon. "*Enchantee, madame,*" he bowed over her hand.

Louisa sidled over to her cousin. "Did you hear him?" she whispered. "He spoke French."

"So do I," Meg whispered back.

Hargrove approached. "May I escort you, Lady Margaret?

"I hope for the pleasure of visiting with you during your stay, Miss Elliott," he added warmly before escorting her cousin in to dine.

"Louisa, can't you hear?" Francis asked.

"Yes? Oh," she reddened deeply. "I was—was wondering how best to proceed," she answered vaguely. "You must listen carefully to all his grace says when the ladies withdraw and you gentlemen share port."

"Why?" Medlock asked, silently wishing he were in London.

Chapter Eleven

Stirring restlessly in the huge Queen Anne four-poster the next morn Louisa became conscious of the delicate fragrance of lavender. A breeze gently stirred the drapes at the open window, deepening the scent.

"Hargrove Retreat," Louisa said aloud, sitting upright. Throwing aside the hand-sewn coverlet she slipped from the deep, down-filled bed and softly padded to the open window. "Lady Thea was right," she mused, a soft smile on her lips. "The lavender beds the sixth Lord Hargrove gave his wife on their first anniversary still bloom. Lord Hargrove has kept them."

She leaned on the windowsill breathing in the aroma from the huge geometric beds in the gardens below. Too soon the tumble of questions, the tenderness endangering her heart descended. She steeled herself against it.

A horse's shrill whiny and thudding hooves caught Louisa's attention. A rider appeared west of the lavender beds near a doric-columned garden house. The covey of servants already scurrying about setting up tables and arranging decorations halted at the sight of the huge stallion. They bowed and tugged at their forelocks in deference to the rider.

"Lord Hargrove." Louisa tried to fuel her resolve. "I wonder that he doesn't have grooms attending him." She watched him lithely dismount, his splendid form amply enhanced by the tight riding breeches and close fitting coat.

Lady Margaret appeared in the connecting doorway, her brow wrinkled with curiosity as she fastened her wrap about her.

Louisa started upright. "Meg, you startled me."

"You were talking and—"

"I saw the duke riding." Louisa turned back to the window. Her heart lurched and cheeks reddened when she saw him doff his hat in greeting. She instinctively retreated.

"It was kind of his grace to give us adjoining rooms," Meg said as she reluctantly joined her at the window. "Are they setting up the tables for a picnic?"

"Lord Hargrove doesn't know what a picnic is." Louisa frowned at the sudden memory of Hargrove and the Frenchman on St. James green. "Do you know where his chambers are?"

Meg teased the lace on her wrap. "Must we do this, Louisa?"

"Not you too?" she blurted. "Last eve Francis refused to tell me what Lord Hargrove said while the gentlemen had their port. Insists he is a bloody 'good fellow.' "

"But there are so many servants who might see us." Lady Margaret wrung her hands. "I wish we were at Hamilton Manor."

"This will be your home if we fail," Louisa reminded her. "Where are his chambers?"

"On the floor below—at the west end. His study is the first room in the west wing," Meg resignedly told her.

Sounds of other horses approaching the garden drew Louisa's gaze. Peering cautiously past the drapery she saw

Hargrove was busy controlling his powerful steed. *How beautifully he handles the beast.*

Does he really mean to betray England? She recognized Lord Brice as one of the riders joining Hargrove. Upon seeing the small dark man with whom Hargrove had spoken in St. James, her heart tumbled. Another man was talking excitedly in French.

The prim abigail hired by the countess for this stay swept into the room. "My lady, an open window will give you a deathly chill. Really, Miss Elliott, you should know better," she said with a curt shake of her finger and then hurried Meg back to her room.

Louisa angrily stamped her foot. The sound of hooves drew her back to the window in time to see Lord Hargrove and his small party ride into the woods beyond the pavilion. *I must stop him,* she thought. She tried to imagine Lord Hargrove at his worst seeking to bank the flames of a far different passion.

Bright golden rays of sunshine streamed through the stained-glass windows of the breakfast room at Hargrove Retreat. Light scattered in bright rainbows about the room. The elegantly tiled fireplace was dark this June morning but the wealth of cavorting hammered-figures in the copper mantel provided its own warmth.

Louisa studied the mantel absentmindedly as she stirred her tea. The delicious pastry before her had cooled. None of the dishes on the Sheraton sideboard tempted her usual good appetite. "No one else seems to have risen yet," she mused, a plan slowly forming.

Meg saw the gleam in her eyes; her heart sank.

"Good morn, my lady. Louisa." Francis bowed stiffly. "May I join you?"

"Of course, Mr. Medlock." Lady Margaret cast a warm

relieved smile, which thawed the young man's awkward formality.

"It's an excellent board," Francis said, as he selected generous portions of kidney pie, ham, beef, eggs, and warm biscuits. Taking a chair opposite the young ladies he signaled the footman to pour his coffee.

He glanced anxiously at Louisa. "What are your plans?"

"Lady Margaret and I were thinking about riding," she answered, ignoring her cousin's soft gasp of dismay at this revelation. She smiled widely thinking that Francis could replace the groom. "Perhaps you would escort us?"

Francis sensed Lady Margaret's distress. "If your ladyship doesn't wish to ride, his grace has other entertainments."

"It's the perfect exercise for Meg," Louisa countered. "As duchess she'll be required to ride in the hunt," she noted matter-of-factly.

"You needn't fear, Meg, I'll order Lord Hargrove's gentlest cob for you." She threw down her napkin, popped from her chair, and strode from the room before Francis could rise.

Flustered, he attacked his kidney pie. He berated himself for succumbing to the countess's lure of manor and lands.

Returning a few minutes later Louisa prattled cheerfully. "All's arranged. I've a promise that you shall be given a lady's steed, Meg. Let's change into our riding habits."

"We'll meet you on the main steps," she told Francis. Taking her reluctant cousin's hand, she drew her forward.

In the corridor Louisa said, "Remember to keep Francis from bolting after me. I must find where Lord Hargrove has gone."

"But it's improper for you to ride alone," Lady Margaret objected worriedly.

"Francis'd never consent to leave you unescorted and you can't keep pace with me. It's the only way," Louisa assured her as she drew on her riding gloves. "Tell Francis I spoke of visiting old Mrs. Porley at Hamilton."

"It'll end in a scold from Grandmama," Meg fretted.

"She can't object to your riding with Francis," Louisa told her. "By Zeus, who could possibly imagine him a threat to your heart?" she laughed.

"Louisa, please, it isn't ladylike to chortle so," Francis chided, joining them at the foot of the huge fan of marble stairs that flared from the center block of Hargrove Retreat.

Grimacing at the reproof, Louisa tripped lightly down the steps. She smiled at the animated black gelding the groom led forward. Eagerly accepting his hand, she vaulted into the sidesaddle.

Once Lady Margaret was atop a placid gray mare and Francis on his own sturdy bay steed, she loosened her reins and led the way across the crushed-gravel square before the Retreat and into the sycamore-lined avenue. A surge of excitement flowed through her. She threw a quick glance over her shoulder and urged the gelding forward, then swerved off the track and through the woods lining the avenue. Francis's shouts to halt spurred her forward.

The woods soon gave way to open fields across low, undulating hills; different stands of trees and shrubs dotted the landscape like dark, green mushrooms.

"It's worse than I feared," Louisa muttered, scanning the horizon. "How'd I think I could stumble across them?" She sighed and then brightened. "I'd best enjoy my freedom, for I won't escape Grandmama again when she learns what I've done." Touching the gelding lightly with her riding crop, she began a leisurely tour. Her opinion of Hargrove as landlord was forced to rise. The land was well tended, the cottagers prosperous, and need for improvements couldn't be found.

Sighting a placid lake surrounded by trees on three sides, Louisa galloped for it. On the near side not far from the

water's edge Louisa spied a fallen tree, perfect for the difficult task of remounting. She prodded the black into the
deeper shade toward the tree. Alerted to someone's approach
by a flock of birds rising from the woods on the opposite
side, Louisa guided her mount behind the fallen tree and
waited.

Hargrove's huge bay burst into the clearing.

"Your Grace! Your Grace!"

The groom haphazardly galloped from the direction she
had just come, startling her. The liveried servant came up to
the duke within her hearing.

"A message, Your Grace. It's urgent—from Mr. Green,"
the lad gasped. "Must see you at once."

"Where?" Hargrove demanded.

"At the Retreat, Your Grace."

"I'll return at once. Retrieve any others sent to find me,"
he ordered and then let the stallion rocket forward.

Unable to catch every word, Louisa had heard "Green"
and "the Retreat." When the groom was out of sight, she
guided her gelding into the open and galloped after
Hargrove.

Topping a hill some time later, Louisa gasped in surprise
at the unexpected sight of the Hargrove Retreat. She
watched Hargrove rein to a halt near the outer, tree-shaded
side of the west wing. He vaulted from his saddle and
slipped through an outer door.

Where has he gone in that behemoth? wondered Louisa
unhappily as she eased her mount down the hill toward the
mansion. *If he's to see Mr. Green it'd surely be in private,*
she reasoned. *In his study—it's in this wing on the second
floor.*

Galloping through the park surrounding the Retreat she
drew her mount to a halt at sight of the first servant. "Please
return my mount to the stables," she said handing the reins

over to a startled gardener. Throwing her bulky riding skirt over her arm, she hurried on, halting when she reached the midsection of the wing. Slowly walking along the wall beneath the trees, she contemplated how to reach his grace's study.

A window above Louisa was pushed open and she caught a glimpse of Hargrove. *I must hear what's being said*, she thought and hurried toward the door he had entered, but found it locked. Louisa glanced up at the open window and saw a squirrel scamper across a branch within inches of the sash.

The solution burst into her mind. A quick survey revealed the tree climbable and the branches plausibly sturdy. In minutes she gained the main split despite the difficulty with her long, heavy riding skirt. Draping this encumbrance over her arm, Louisa climbed up the tree until she reached the larger of the two branches that grew in front of the window. She maneuvered slowly around the trunk and onto the branch, using her free hand on the higher branch to balance herself.

Words floated from the window but were too faint to be clear. After glancing down, Louisa edged toward the window. The heel of one of her riding boots caught in the crotch of a small offshoot, throwing her off-balance. She wavered, dropped her skirts and grabbed hold of the branch above her with her other hand.

Inside his study, Lord Hargrove contemplated the news Green had given him. Staring abstractedly out the window he became aware of a strangely wavering branch. He rose, his eyes fixed on it. "It was uncommon calm when I entered," he muttered.

"Calm? What has that to do with anything?" Green questioned.

"We appear to have a particularly gusty wind of a sudden." His grace casually extracted a silver-handled dueling pistol from one of the drawers of his desk.

"Your Grace?" Green started nervously rising.

Hargrove signaled him to remain still and stole to the window. Thrusting his torso out the window, hand raised, he centered the pistol on the intruder. "Good God!"

"My lord!" Louisa gasped, staring into the threatening muzzle.

"What is it, Your Grace? Is someone actually outside the window?" Mr. Green asked.

"What? Nothing," Hargrove said. "Nothing but a gust of wind." He forced a foolish laugh, clasped an arm about the man and moved him away from the window. "It's thoughtless of me not to let you refresh yourself. My butler will show you to a room. We'll continue in a half hour."

"But Your Grace, this is most urgent."

"A few minutes'll not harm our planning." Lord Hargrove opened the study's door and gently shoved the hapless man out. Closing it sharply, he snapped the bolt in place and strode back to the window.

"By that ogre Napoleon, what're you doing?" he demanded.

"Returning a fallen sparrow to its nest?" Louisa posed hopefully, attempting to smile despite her predicament.

"There are *no* nests in this tree."

A blush surged from her collar to her now askew riding hat. Trying to edge back, Louisa's foot slipped off the branch. She hung precariously for a moment, then regained her footing. Her throat closed with fear and she froze.

"For God's sake, don't move again," Hargrove said. His heart had slammed into his ribs when she slipped. "I'll have a ladder brought around immediately."

"No!"

Louisa's heart-rending cry halted him.

"I'd rather fall. Grandmama would—" She turned her face away, unable to bear his gaze.

Understanding her fear, he said more gently, "You can't remain there." He weighed the options. *Madness*, he cursed.

"I'll be back in an instant—and alone," he told her and dashed from the study to his chambers down the corridor. Tearing into the room he astonished his valet by wrenching open cabinet doors and strewing their contents.

"Ah ha!" Hargrove exclaimed, unearthing his dress sword. Taking it, he scooped up the black satin ceremonial sash. "Sorry, Wards," he said rushing past the unbelieving valet.

A passing footman dared a quizzical gaze but hurried on his way at the duke's scowl.

Louisa gasped at the sword in Hargrove's hand. "What do you mean to do with that?"

"Just seeing if it was long enough," Lord Hargrove answered, surveying the situation with a critical eye.

"For what? Am I to be run through?"

"It's a thought," he answered, his grin belying the words as he wrapped one end of the sash about his wrist. "Being a gentleman I must save you first."

Louisa gaped at him, puzzled as he tied one end of the sash about his wrist, thrust the point of the sword through the other end, then held it out to her.

"Take hold of the sash with one hand," Keane commanded. He leaned further out of the window. "Take it. Good. Wrap it tightly about your hand. That's right. Now, step toward me. Steady. Stop," he halted her at the sound of a telltale creak.

"Come forward as fast as you dare. If you begin to fall, grab hold the sash with both hands," he instructed and leaned as far out the window as he dared. "Ready?"

Louisa gulped, trying to still her chattering teeth and nodded. A low, ominous snap propelled her forward. Inches from Hargrove's grasp, the branch gave way. She lunged, realizing there was nothing but space below her.

Lord Hargrove grabbed for her, his heart lurching to his throat. He caught Louisa's hand. In moments he had pulled her up and through the window.

Clinging to Hargrove, Louisa gasped for air, unaware that his arms were wrapped thankfully about her. Relief slowly loosened fright's hold and she looked up. A tremor coursed through her.

"I should never have let you attempt it," Lord Hargrove admonished himself. "You might've been killed." His arms tightened protectively, then abruptly loosened.

"What *were* you doing out there?" he demanded with ducal hauteur. She cringed back and he stopped the scold.

"I—I was—curious." Louisa could not bear his piercing gaze. "Thank you for—for not calling anyone." She looked up, then down quickly. His embrace—so strong, so comforting rocked her. His scent filled her mind with a luscious vision. Trembling, she groaned.

"Are you hurt? Bruised?" Lord Hargrove loosened his hold and ran his hands down her arms.

"No. No," she repeated and backed away until the black satin sash halted her.

Both looked at it, still tied about Lord Hargrove's wrist and tightly wrapped about Louisa's hand. Their eyes ran along it and up to each other's gaze.

The world disappeared in the breathless moment. They stepped toward one another, exchanged a gentle kiss that was deepening.

"Your Grace? Your Grace, is everything all right?" Talbot demanded outside the study's door.

Louisa gasped. Her features flamed bright red and then pallid white.

"Louisa," Keane implored as she pulled away.

"Your Grace?" the butler called insistently.

"Dismiss everyone in the corridor and bring Mr. Green to the library," Lord Hargrove spoke with a false calm, an inner turmoil tearing at his heart at he stared at Louisa's back.

"A few moments after I go, Louisa, leave this room. We shall speak later," he told her, with an unspoken plea for understanding. He reached out but dropped his hand when she trembled at his touch. Realizing he could only make matters worse, Hargrove gathered up hope from what he had read in her eyes in that precious moment before they kissed and Talbot interrupted them. He withdrew, gently closing the door.

Part of Louisa screamed to call him back. An alarming, terrifying truth had flashed into her consciousness. She had stepped toward him, kissed of her own volition. "No," she whispered, wrapping her arms protectively about herself. "No."

Chapter Twelve

Francis glanced anxiously at Lady Margaret. "Perhaps we should escort Louisa from Mrs. Porley's?"

"No," she swallowed her distress. "Louisa manages quite well. It's a kind thought." She smiled shyly.

"But Countess Tember is certain to—"

"It's a worry," Lady Margaret agreed, sighing heavily. She reined her plodding mare to a halt and patted his arm reassuringly. Their gazes met. Held.

Francis's gelding shifted, breaking the spell. The young man cleared his throat with a nervous start. "If you say not, then we'll not," he managed at last, his face uncomfortably warm. Not daring to glance at her with his heart pounding so, he urged his bay forward.

A sorrowful understanding weighed heavily upon Meg. If there'd been any doubt where her heart lay, that gaze had ended it. To see her affection could be returned added to her desperate determination to do what was right for all concerned. "You mustn't think harshly of Louisa," she said when she caught up with Francis. "She's not a scapegrace."

Doubtfully arching a brow, Francis looked at the fragile

102

beauty. She was only an arm's span away but less attainable than a coronet. "You're too good, my lady," he murmured.

"You mustn't say that, Mr. Medlock." Lady Margaret gripped her reins tightly. "Louisa has never been unkind to me. I don't know what I'd have done without her comfort after my father's death." Tears of frustration, guilt and despair burst their dam.

The catch in her voice alerted Francis. He took hold of her mount's reins. "You mustn't distress yourself, my lady," he protested. "I hold Miss Elliott in—in high regard," the young man declared. He dismounted with far greater grace than anyone could have imagined. "Let me help you down."

Meg nodded, daintily dabbed at her eyes, and tried to marshal her resolution. Putting her hands on Francis's shoulders, she marveled at the ease with which he lifted her.

"My lady," Francis breathed huskily, his hands lingering on her waist. Desperate hope and haunting helplessness jumbled.

A small, tight sob broke from Meg. She covered her face with her hands, leaned against his chest, the battle momentarily lost.

Francis cradled her gently, recklessness flowing through him at her warmth in his arms. He savored the long moment, easing her hold only when her tears had ceased. "Dare I hope?" he began, unable to halt the words.

"You mustn't," Lady Margaret shook her head sadly. "You must forget this." Her gaze pleaded for understanding then she stepped back, turning away. "It's my foolish sensibilities—overset by a restless night, Mr. Medlock." She tried to lighten her tone, "That's all it was."

After blowing her nose in her kerchief she faced him once again. "You were—were kind to endure such sheepish behavior. You needn't fear such a—an unseemly display from my cousin," Meg finished more steadily. She met his gaze. "It's true she's skittish and her behavior startling at times, but it's always prompted by her efforts to help others. She has a kind heart, Mr. Medlock." She walked slowly back to her mount.

Francis swallowed the praises bursting in his heart. *What a brave, beautiful lady*, he thought, but realized he must follow her dictates. Lifting her back onto the sidesaddle he gazed lovingly at her finely shaped features, the golden curls.

"My grandmother is set on a match with Lord Hargrove," Lady Margaret told him, carefully arranging the reins in her gloved hands while Francis remounted. "He—doesn't seem adverse to it and I've never known Grandmama to fail."

"I know," he answered hollowly, her courage steadying him. "I think it best we return to the Retreat." Francis motioned for her to proceed.

Lady Margaret broke the silence some time later. "You'll find Louisa has an excellent seat."

Francis forced a smile. "Has she never startled you?"

"No," Meg answered with a gentle laugh. "But my heart has trembled. It's not a dull life one leads with Louisa."

Francis sighed heavily. "I fear she strongly dislikes my irresoluteness," he admitted.

Meg stiffened in her saddle, her eyes suddenly blazing. "Don't speak so, Mr. Medlock. You display a gentlemanly restraint. Louisa feels the same, I assure you. She's merely—shy in expressing her feelings." Meg colored beneath his doubting smile. *It's best*, she assured herself. *Louisa will come to see his worth and love him. She must.*

Moler's dark eyes narrowed. "I can't tarry much longer. Each day increases the danger of discovery."

Hargrove stood before the small man, his distaste carefully concealed. "Word arrived this morn that the final document shall arrive soon. Perhaps by morning."

"All these people about—it's most unwise."

"I take the greater risk, *monsieur,*" Hargrove said curtly. "Can you fulfill your part of our agreement?"

"It'd be foolish to answer, Your Grace," the Frenchman laughed derisively. "What would there be to stop you from turning me over to the Admiralty and claiming the gold?"

"Until you deliver the documents you must trust me, *n'est-ce pas*? Just as I must rely upon your 'English' honor," he taunted. Moler grinned and rose. "My patience and generosity aren't limitless, Your Grace—just as your funds have proven." He bowed mockingly.

"With your permission I'll use a mount in the morn."

"Of course," Lord Hargrove nodded. His gaze followed the small man as he left the library.

A short time later Lady Badden entered. She fanned her face demurely, posing deftly, her high-waisted gown giving the allusion of translucence. "It's very gracious of you to include Lord Badden and me in your party."

"How else was I to enjoy your company?" Hargrove asked, sauntering to her side with an appreciative gleam in his eye. "I hope you're enjoying your stay." He took her hand and wished with all his heart this business was done.

Her free hand stole up his arm and about his neck. Lady Badden drew his head down, her eyes flashing a passionate invitation. "Last eve you promised to show me the famous lavender beds." She twined a finger in his fair hair.

Hargrove drew her to him, his kiss harsh.

Fluttering in his arms, triumph gleamed in Lady Badden's eyes. Moving deftly away, she smiled. "You overwhelm me, Your Grace. It wouldn't do for Lady Margaret to discover our *tendre* for one another."

Hargrove grimaced.

"Your Grace," Lady Angela Badden batted her lashes coquettishly, swayed out of his reach. "You're an abominable man." She ran a finger along his cheek and sighed.

Hargrove raised her chin. "This eve?"

Lady Badden sighed regretfully. She stiffened at the sound of steps in the corridor.

Both turned to the door, a scowl creasing Hargrove's features when he saw Francis Medlock. "Yes?" he asked curtly.

Francis bowed stiffly. "Lady Margaret awaits you in the gardens," he said abruptly, his eyes going accusingly to Lady Badden before he stalked away.

Viscount Brice strolled into the library a moment later. "What has given young Medlock such a black look?" He arched a brow at the sight of Lady Badden. "If I'm interrupting—"

"Of course not, Lord Brice." She fluttered her fan. "We must chat later, Your Grace," she curtsied lowly and glided away.

"Any closer to success?" Brice asked.

Hargrove frowned in distaste. "What'd you learn?"

"Moler met two gentlemen this morn after he left us. Near Colchester." The viscount carefully closed the library's doors. "I followed them to Brightling Sea where they went aboard a sloop. They came ashore with two large portmanteaus."

"Where are they now?"

"At the Crossed Arms."

"Then we've but to await Green's man." Lord Hargrove poured two glasses of brandy and handed one to Lord Brice. "It can't be done soon enough," he said and quaffed his.

"I'd never attempt three courtships," Glynn offered caustically.

"I wish you were a Hargrove," Lord Hargrove said with subdued bitterness, his thoughts on Louisa, so soft and unknowingly alluring in his arms. "The coronet may yet cost me all that matters."

Chapter Thirteen

"We're dining outdoors this eve—how delightful," Lady Angela Badden purred softly as she passed Hargrove who was standing with her husband before the Pavilion in the gardens. With a regretful glance at the duke, she joined the Countess Tember, Lady Edwina and the Marchioness Grenby.

The countess glared at the diaphanous gown, which she was certain, had been dampened. "Aren't you fearful that you'll take a chill?"

"Lord Hargrove has such distinctive tastes," Lady Badden ignored the censure, and addressed Lady Thea. "You must take much pleasure in guiding him," she simpered.

"His inclination since my arrival is singular, but not, unfortunately, admirable," the marchioness said reprovingly.

The smile froze on Lady Badden's lips. "A delightful eve," she murmured, and sauntered away.

"A shameless creature." The countess scowled. "To have invited her and my Margaret," she harrumphed loudly. "A word concerning discretion is necessary to his grace, Lady Thea."

"Lord Hargrove's no longer a child." The marchioness

looked at her cousin's snug white breeches and dark jacket, a silk embroidered waistcoat the only note of subdued elegance. "There's a reason for Lady Badden's presence other than the obvious."

Recognizing a rebuff, Countess Tember didn't challenge her. "Where are Lady Margaret and Louisa?" she demanded irritably. "Edwina, you should've remained with them until their toilettes were complete."

"They'll appear in a few moments," Lady Edwina said quietly.

Catching her eye, Lady Thea smiled graciously. "I recall that you have an interest in gardening, Lady Edwina. Isn't the Retreat's garden magnificent? Capability Brown began the work but Keane has done much. The gardens have won him an invitation to participate in the new National Horticultural Society."

Brightening visibly at mention of her favorite hobby, Lady Edwina nodded agreement with the honor. An attractive glow lit her features. "We're indebted to Mr. Wedgewood for seeing the necessity of such an organization. They're to begin an experimental garden in Kensington."

Countess Tember flicked her fan open. "What nonsense are you prattling about?"

"Do excuse us, my lady," the marchioness rose and drew Edwina with her. "I must introduce your daughter to Lord Cearcy. He arrived only this afternoon. He's a close friend of Mr. Hatchard and is instrumental in the Horticultural Society."

She pointed out a distinguished gentleman joining Hargrove. His figure was attractive, the gray dappling of his dark hair the only sign that five and forty was his age.

The countess followed them, tempering her frown into a smile when they joined the gentlemen. While introductions were being made, Countess Tember laid a hand on Hargrove's arm and interrupted. "We'll leave you to your greenery. Lord Hargrove is going to favor me with a stroll," she said, tightening her hold.

Hargrove nodded, a wry grimace answering his cousin's glance.

"Come along," Countess Tember impatiently drew him away. "We must speak," she began when out of everyone's hearing.

"Indeed, it's imperative."

The countess cocked her head inquisitively. "Then, let's begin. First, I must ask your indulgence, your understanding that an old woman's affection for her granddaughter prompts these questions. I offer no offense."

"Where none is warranted, none shall be."

"It's a most delicate matter. Rumors abound in London concerning your financial difficulties." She looked at him hopefully.

"Yes?"

"You don't protest?"

"To the rumors or your prying?"

"Your Grace," the countess began, her cheeks a dull red.

"You wish to withdraw consideration of marriage?" Hargrove asked impassively.

"The question is prompted by concern for my grand-daughter's future. You must understand that I wish more than your uncle's reassurance?" Countess Tember blustered. "It's far too late for you to withdraw."

"I assure you, I intend to wed your *granddaughter*."

"But the dowry's almost been agreed upon—" she halted. "What did you say?"

"I don't have your permission?" Lord Hargrove casually flicked an invisible fleck from his sleeve.

"I—well—you must realize that she's very young," she stammered.

"I mean to court your granddaughter. To win her affection

before any marriage," he answered, starring at the mirror-surface of the lake in his gardens.

Countess Tember regained her composure. "Your words are at odds with appearances. But I've lived long in this world and understand such matters," she added condescendingly.

"Then I've your approval?"

"If you win my granddaughter's affection it must be given, Your Grace. You've my blessing."

"Thank you, my lady," Lord Hargrove smiled widely. "May I rely on your discretion?"

"Of course," she assured him, her triumph barely concealed. Hargrove's obvious satisfaction convinced the countess of absolute success.

Sitting to one side in the salon after dining, Louisa watched Keane turn the pages for Lady Margaret as she played the pianoforte. She still seethed with arguments and counter-arguments, which had been battling with each other ever since their encounter in the study. Each scene since their first meeting was examined, searched for a clue of how he had stolen her heart.

He is very handsome, she thought, *but what has dealt my heart this blow? He is haughty, arrogant*— Hargrove having raised his head, their eyes met and her thought faded. She flicked her fan open angrily, looking away.

Am I a simple dalliance? A blush stole to her cheeks at the memory of his kisses. *Why didn't I resist? How could I be so easily seduced?*

Her gaze went to the other men. Lord Brice was equally handsome but her heart didn't rise to her throat at thought of him taking her hand. Seeing her grandmother, Louisa shivered.

A high-pitched chortle caught Louisa's attention and she looked to see Lord Badden steady his wife. *Such an ill-*

made match, she thought. *Will Meg be unhappy and take to drink and flirting as Lady Badden has?* She flitted her fan furiously.

Francis said quietly, "Would you like to take a stroll?"

"Do go, Louisa," the countess waved permission. "Don't remain too long." The pair forgotten she leaned to Lady Thea.

"Wasn't that delightful. They make a splendid couple."

Seeing Hargrove take Meg's arm, Louisa propelled Francis onto the veranda. His treading on her skirt halted her.

"I—I am sorry." Medlock hurriedly removed his foot. "I don't think it is torn," he added, brushing at the stain.

"Let it be." Angered by her harshness, she took his arm and walked forward. Silence hung heavy. "Francis, I don't know what we are to do." Stumbling, she reached out.

Francis steadied her.

"Raspberries," Louisa swore, fighting back tears. "Can't we even take a walk without encountering disaster."

Francis gazed at her regretfully. "I know you do—don't approve of me."

"That's not true." Tears rimmed her eyes. *Is Grandmother right after all? Am I hopeless?* "It's this wretched match."

"I regret that it's so distasteful to you," Francis said dismally, his hands dropping away.

Utter dejection flickered across her features. "You misunderstand—"

" "Couldn't we be friends?" Medlock asked lowly.

"Oh, Francis." Tears spilled down her cheeks.

Medlock wrapped her in a brotherly embrace, awkwardly patting her back. "It can't be so terrible."

"We should be able to see Mr. Medlock and your cousin," Lord Hargrove said lightly as he and Lady Margaret stepped out onto the veranda. "I haven't had much opportunity to visit with either." His companion trembled. "Should I send for a wrap?"

"No, it's not that cool but I think we should return to the salon," Lady Margaret answered agitatedly.

His eyes flicked past her. The silhouette of Louisa in Medlock's arms twisted his heart.

Drawing back, Louisa summoned a weak smile. "I'm usually not so missish."

"You needn't fear I think ill of you," Francis said with a sigh of relief at her regained composure. "I wanted to apologize, to tell you I changed my mind. I want to help prove Hargrove's unsuitability," he ended hurriedly, his color rising beneath her searching look.

"You've discovered the Frenchman," Louisa exclaimed. She quickly told of the refusal of one of the duke's servants to speak of the man. "Do you know anything that can be used?"

Louisa finished, caught between hope and fear.

Francis shook his head, reluctant to reveal the scene in the library with Lady Badden. "Nothing useful. But there must be some way, something we can discover to dissuade the countess. I'm certain Lady Margaret has no desire to wed Lord Hargrove," he ended, bitterly.

"Has she spoken of it?" Louisa asked in amazement.

"She's far too kind, too circumspect."

"She'll never naysay Grandmama."

"It'd be a splendid match if he loved her," Francis defended Lady Margaret. "He is, after all, a duke."

Louisa clenched her hands. "At the Devonshire ball Meg said Lord Hargrove reacted guiltily when Lord Devonshire spoke of missing government documents. That same eve I witnessed a meeting between Lord Hargrove and a Mr. Green of the War Department. Mr. Green is now here at the Retreat. I bet Moler is here to receive the missing documents."

"A strong accusation but weak evidence." Francis said.

"Then we must contrive to watch him as I suggested last eve," Louisa bolstered her determination. "Perhaps we could take turns watching the duke so that he doesn't become suspicious."

"I think it'd be far wiser, if not safer, to watch Moler," Francis said nervously. "We're not suited to this."

"Do you have a better plan?" Louisa challenged.

"No," Francis shook his head.

"But you don't believe that you and I can succeed," Louisa said with the force of her pent-up emotions. "Shall we abandon Meg? Retreat?"

"Never," Francis said firmly. "Even if I must call the duke out on the field of honor."

"Let's hope that doesn't come to pass," she said more calmly. "He'd be your death. That wouldn't please Meg.

"Let's not be hasty, Francis." She took his arm and began walking back to the veranda. "Let's watch and pray he makes an error. Mine is already done," she ended in an aside.

"What?"

"A fool's mutterings," she laughed hollowly. "I'll not return to the salon. Please tell Grandmama that I've the headache. Perhaps I can think of a more successful scheme."

"May God speed," Francis said and with a bow walked away.

Louisa shook her head. *Whatever has gotten into him?* she wondered. She thought of Meg and then of Keane. *Surely this is but a foolish infatuation*, she weakly assured herself.

Chapter Fourteen

"It's an abomination," Countess Tember disclaimed loudly. "How can Pitt allow such an outrage?" she repeated.

"He'd hardly have been consulted," Lady Thea objected, reluctantly following the countess into the Retreat's entry hall.

"Those poor men, it's too ghastly," Lady Margaret remarked.

"See that our parcels are placed in our rooms," Countess Tember imperiously ordered the butler.

The marchioness's glance as she drew off her gloves prevented his objection. "Where's his grace, Talbot?"

"In the library with the other gentlemen, my lady."

The countess strode past Lady Thea. "They'll wish to have this news."

Lady Margaret winced at this blatant usurpation of place, but it showed that her grandmother must be very sure of the match.

Lady Thea took her arm and flashed an understanding smile.

Louisa came down the stairs as the pair passed. "Did I hear Grandmama? Did you find the ribbons you wanted, Meg?"

114

Lady Margaret's eyes widened. "I completely forgot about them. The news in Colchester was too terrible."

"Come with us," Lady Thea told Louisa. "The countess is about to reveal what we heard to the gentlemen."

"We agree that it's insupportable," Lord Cearcy finished as the ladies entered. "Now tell us what you are talking about."

"The French have executed eight Englishmen." The countess's voice shook. "Eight."

Louisa's gaze flashed to Keane.

"They claim they were spies," the countess continued. "It was an excuse. Pitt must be forced to take action."

"The gentlemen knew their lives would be forfeit," Lord Brice offered. "Death awaits spies and traitors."

Louisa took hold her cousin's arm to steady herself.

"Are you all right?" Meg whispered.

"Just shock," Louisa returned, willing her legs steady.

"Leave the room if you can't be silent, Louisa," the countess demanded.

Her cheeks reddened like ripe cherries, and then paled stark white at the pitying glances cast her way. Louisa fled.

"Such a hopeless child," the countess grumbled. "I don't know how Medlock shall ever manage her." She had a vision of him bolting back to London. "Where is he?"

"Mr. Medlock went riding," Hargrove answered tersely. "You should go to your chamber and rest, my lady." He guided the countess toward the door. "The news has overset you."

"I'll assist her," Lady Margaret said, awed that her grandmother had been rendered speechless.

Lord Badden excused himself from the awkward scene.

"I must visit with the gardener about the new hibiscus you ordered from Italy," Lord Cearcy said and followed him.

Lord Hargrove turned to his cousin when they had gone. "Thea, was there other news?"

"Rumors that the French are intensifying their search for spies; others that the marines have tightened their patrols off the coast to ensure no French spies succeed in going to France."

Viscount Brice and Hargrove shared an understanding glance.

"Is there something you wish to tell us?" Lady Thea asked as she walked to her husband's side.

"See to your wife's imagination, Grenby," Hargrove said smiling. "It's enough I must bear Countess Tember's impertinence.

"Speaking of which, I had best find Miss Elliott. Glynn?" he motioned his friend to follow and left without further word.

Lady Thea posed a finger on her chin. "Isn't that odd?"

"Now, my dear," Lord Grenby began.

"But it was odd how the news affected Miss Elliott. I mean before her grandmother spoke," his wife continued. "It's a ghastly business, but she knew none of the men."

The marquess shrugged. "Women are oft over-sensitive about such matters."

"I'm positive she imagined Keane blindfolded and about to be executed when Lord Brice spoke of death to spies and traitors." She shook her fiery curls. "I dislike it."

Lord Brice halted in the corridor. "This'll mean trouble."

"The countess need never know I—"

"Countess?" The viscount put a hand on Hargrove's shoulder and pushed him through a door to their right. "Listen, old man, you can't go mooning about like a lad in his first calf-love. I was speaking of the executions." His features deepened with a worried scowl.

"Just how you ever thought to juggle Lady Badden, the countess, Miss Elliott, and our 'business' is beyond reason."

Hargrove's eyes flashed angrily. "What would you have me do?"

"Make some excuse to get everyone out of here. Come down with the small pox," Brice said exasperatedly.

"I can't do that." Lord Hargrove clamped his jaws stubbornly.

The viscount paused. "What of Lady Badden?" he demanded.

"Has she taken the bait?"

Hargrove grimaced.

"It's too late to cry off now, Keane."

"I know. Trust me to do my part." Anger darkened his eyes. "Let me do it in my way." He passed a hand across his face, taking in a deep breath and then slowly exhaling. "Glynn, I know this is not the best way but—"

"You'd better be after Miss Elliott," the viscount said grimly. "Settle your issue with her where Lady Badden can't see you. I've no desire to explain this to the War Department should we fail."

Flashing a smile of gratitude, Keane left him.

"Why, there you are." Lady Badden swayed to Hargrove's side. "I was *very* disappointed that you neglected me last eve." She leaned heavily on his arm.

"Grenby was difficult," Lord Hargrove lied smoothly.

"How unfortunate," she pouted. "But I'll forgive you." She brushed his cheek with a kiss.

Hargrove stepped back. "Be more circumspect, Angela,"

"That old harridan Tember has put you out of sorts," Lady Badden said drawing him forward. "Let us go to the gallery. It is quite devoid of visitors," she offered seductively. "Ah, here we are."

Lord Hargrove frowned in the darkness and then took her in his arms and kissed her.

"Your Grace," Lady Badden drew back breathless.

"You're a man of contradictions." She moved away. "How am I to believe you love me when you dally after the Hamilton chit day and night?"

"She is only a convenient solution for me, my love," Lord Hargrove answered. "You shouldn't be jealous of a green girl."

"What 'solution' could she possibly offer you, Your Grace?"

Hargrove suddenly dropped his hold. "Will you leave me no pride, my lady?"

"What has pride to do in this?" A note of uncertainty crept into her words. She reached out and touched his arm.

"I must wed the Hamilton chit."

"The rumors? They are true?" Lady Badden gasped. "But your gifts to me—how can your fortune be gone?"

"Not gone, but in great need of assistance. I beg of you to be patient."

"The Hamiltons can't have enough wealth for the purpose," she resisted. "Is *that* why Moler is here?"

Hope for success calmed Hargrove. "How do you know him?"

"I saw him once—with a friend," she answered hastily.

"He's a friend of Brice's." He frowned as if displeased. "What is your interest in the man?" he asked sullenly, feigning jealousy.

Lady Badden caressed his cheek. "You needn't fear on that account.

"If I were to show you a way to regain your fortune—to pay your debts, wouldn't you be grateful, Lord Hargrove?" she asked, leaning toward him. "Grateful enough to make me your duchess?"

He gazed at her, his true feelings well-hidden. "If it could be done, I'd be eternally beholden to you."

"What would you be willing to do to achieve it?" she

asked softly. "Think on it. If your nerves aren't too weak, meet me in the morn and we shall go riding."

"Are you serious?" he half-laughed.

"Terribly so."

"Then tell me now," Hargrove asked eagerly but not for the reason Lady Badden supposed.

"Someone is calling for you," she said.

"What? I hear them," Hargrove swore angrily. "Go at once. We'll speak in the morn. Till then—my love."

After a few moments, Lady Badden peered into the corridor. Finding it empty, she also departed.

The Hargrove ancestors stared from their canvases in the gallery's muted light. But Louisa did not see them as she edged from behind the heavy damask curtain opposite the door.

"You must eat something," Meg urged her cousin to take the broth that had been brought to her room. "It can't help Francis for you to fret so. You must have been dreadfully overset by the news to faint. I was certain the servants had told you—you looked so different when you joined us," she prattled on nervously.

"It may be just as they say. Francis's mount was frightened and he lost his seat and the steed returned home on its own," she said trying to bolster her own spirits as well as Louisa's.

"Did you see Moler at all today?" Louisa asked hollowly.

"Who? Oh, the dark Frenchman. I haven't seen him except for that morn in the garden with his grace." Lady Margaret raised a spoon of broth. "Please eat before Grandmama comes."

Louisa pushed the spoon aside. "It's my doing that Francis is lost. He said we were not suited to this task."

A knock on the door sounded.

"There you are, Lady Margaret," Lady Edwina said fluttering into the room after knocking. "The countess wishes you to come down at once." She patted Louisa's hand. "I'll come back to you as soon as we finish dining."

"Have you learned anything more about Fran—Mr. Medlock?" Lady Margaret asked tremulously.

"They were unable to find him." She shook her head. "The duke said nothing more can be done until the morn. We can only hope poor Mr. Medlock has not come to a bad end.

"Why, child, you are faint," Lady Edwina gasped, steadying Meg.

Louisa clambered out of the bed and took the bowl of broth from her cousin's shaking hands. "What is it?"

"The countess warned you to eat at luncheon." Lady Edwina clicked her tongue nervously.

"And you have been urging *me* to eat," Louisa scolded lightly, relieved to see Meg's color returning.

"I'm fine," Lady Margaret protested weakly.

Lady Edwina hesitated a moment, and then thinking of her niece's fate if she did not come down for supper said, "We must hurry. Your abigail has your gown laid out. Come along," she drew her to the connecting doors.

"I'm going to join you," Louisa threw after them.

"Oh, dear. Do you think that wise?" her aunt halted in mid-step. "The countess—"

"Grandmama won't be happy if Meg is late," Louisa vanquished any further protest. "If I'm to find Francis and save Meg from that—that libertine, I can't cower in my room," she muttered. *His grace will learn that not all the Hamiltons grovel before his coronet.*

"Why, Miss Elliott, this is a pleasant surprise," Lady Thea greeted her at the salon door.

"My cousin will join us in a few moments," Louisa told her. Her eyes flashed challengingly at Lord Hargrove's approach.

"May I add to Lady Thea's praise of your rapid recovery?" Louisa snapped open her fan. "Dare I prevent you?"

Hargrove drew in a sharp breath. "Mr. Medlock's disappearance has overset you, Miss Elliott."

"It should overset *you*."

"What nonsense are you prattling, Louisa?" Countess Tember joined them. "You must forgive her, Your Grace."

"You misread your granddaughter's intent," Lord Hargrove answered, studying Louisa with ill-concealed puzzlement.

"Grandmama errs only in her judgment of you, Your Grace," she returned archly.

"And here is Lady Margaret," Lady Thea exclaimed in relief. "We were just about to go into supper," she said loudly and secured Lord Hargrove's arm.

"Why, Meg, you're wearing great-grandmama's pearls." Louisa turned to the duke.

"They are priceless, Your Grace. How many duns will their sale satisfy?" she asked, snapping her fan shut.

"Perhaps you would wish to continue this conversation in private," Hargrove said, his hauteur firmly in place.

"No doubt you would prefer that." She met his gaze and her resolution faltered.

"We must lead, cousin," Lady Thea drew Hargrove forward. "Miss Elliott has made a remarkable recovery," she noted lowly when he seated her. "What have you done to raise her bile?"

"She is a 'singular' young woman, Thea, whom you'll enjoy getting to know. She, too, does not see my consequence."

"You should warn Lady Badden. Miss Elliott is about to—" Rending material and a cry of alarm interrupted her, "to lose a flounce." She swallowed a smile at Louisa's profuse apology and Lady Badden's angry exit.

"Beware, cousin. I do believe the signal has been raised for a full charge against you."

Chapter Fifteen

The countess strode into Louisa's room, great agitation evident. "Never have I been so humiliated," she said lividly. "And you haven't even the grace to profess regret. How dare you use your impertinent tongue on Lord Hargrove?" Countess Tember demanded.

"No, Grandmama."

"*Now* she has nothing to say." The countess threw her hands up. "Perhaps you'd rather tread on my skirt," she said sarcastically. "Lady Badden may be a shameless strumpet set upon cuckolding her husband, but at least she can walk through a room without wrecking havoc."

Hurrying to the countess from the connecting door, Lady Margaret implored, "Grandmama, please."

"It'll do no good to plead for your cousin," Countess Tember said, folding her arms. "If I didn't have Lord Hargrove's word that he'll wed you, you'd be receiving a severe scold for your behavior."

Meg blanched. "His word," she repeated breathlessly.

"Yes, but don't let that put your mind at ease, my dear. If you continue your milk and toast ways he could well regret that decision." She shook her finger beneath Meg's nose. "Your actions this eve could have destroyed my dreams had I not brought his grace to the mark before times."

The countess rounded on Louisa. "As soon as is possible, without causing further comment, you'll go to Hamilton Manor. If young Medlock is found, you'll be wed at once. If not—"

"Grandmama, don't say it." Lady Margaret burst into tears.

"See what you've caused," Countess Tember snapped angrily at Louisa. "Come, my dear. Your sensibilities are too overwrought." She wrapped an arm about her weeping grand-daughter. "True quality is always thus," she flung over her shoulder as she guided Lady Margaret back to her chamber.

Louisa stared at the closed door for long minutes trying to keep back threatening tears. *Oh, Grandmama, won't you ever love me?* She sat on the bed battling the hurt.

Keane, why are you doing this? Burying her face in a pillow, her tears flowed.

"Louisa. Louisa?"

The meek call slowly filtered through to her conscious-ness. The touch of a hand on her shoulder awakened her.

"I didn't mean to frighten you." Meg stood like a specter at her bedside.

She sat up, realized she'd fallen asleep without disrobing. "What's wrong?"

"Everything's wrong," Meg sobbed and fell into her cousin's arms.

"It can't be so dreadful," Louisa patted her gently. "Here, take my kerchief."

Lady Margaret obediently accepted it and daintily dabbed at her red-rimmed eyes. "It's far more terrible than you can imagine," she sniffed loudly.

"Grandmama gave you a scold?"

"No, she said that I'd be a duchess soon." A fresh burst of tears poured forth. Gulping them back Meg took a deep breath. "I have thought and thought about what you would do, Louisa, and—and I decided I cannot marry Lord Hargrove.

"I tried to tell Grandmama that I wouldn't, but she kept repeating how he meant to court me, how much he cared for me, and how wonderful it'd be for us when I am his duchess." She wrung her hands. "How I wish I had your courage."

"No, you don't," Louisa smiled wryly. "My 'courage' has gotten Francis kidnapped or worse. I'm certain he was following Moler as we had planned."

"Then—then he may be—" All color drained from Lady Margaret's features. Her hands fluttered to her breast.

"Why, Meg," Louisa said, struck by a thunderbolt idea. "You are in love with Francis!"

Lady Margaret's lip trembled. She gave a slight nod.

"Why didn't you tell me?" Louisa exclaimed. "It'd have been so easy. It still can be."

"Do not be so cruel." Meg tried to rise.

"Wait. Don't you see what this means? Francis certainly loves you. It explains his sudden eagerness to aid me. His love for you is stronger than his fear of either Grandmama or Lord Hargrove." She shook her head. "No wonder you were constantly singing his praises."

"Francis did try so hard to please you," Meg sniffed. "And you were unkind to him."

"Monstrously," she agreed. "If he were here you could elope."

"Louisa!"

"It'd be the perfect solution."

"But Grandmama? It'd upset her dreadfully."

"Francis hasn't yet been found, so we'll argue about it later," Louisa placated her.

"You said Francis followed Moler. Why would he have kidnapped Francis?"

"Most likely because something was discovered. If only I knew where to look for him."

"What of Lord Hargrove? Surely he wouldn't take part in such a—" she began.

Louisa shook her head. "I don't know what to think about him, not after what I've heard."

"Why were you saying such provoking things to his grace this eve?" She laid a hand on Louisa's. "You were in such a taking. *And* you never stumbled. Lady Badden was no accident." Lady Margaret half-grinned.

"Why do you dislike her?" She looked calculatingly at Louisa. "Is it because she always flirts with Lord Hargrove?"

"What nonsense," Louisa snorted. "As if I give a thought to that. It's merely my awkwardness," she insisted, but wasn't able to meet Meg's gaze.

"I've seen you watch Lord Hargrove. And once I saw a fondness in his gaze when it rested upon you," Lady Margaret persisted.

"Don't babble so, Meg," Louisa snapped, frowning. "He can't know what true affection is."

"How can you say that? He's been very kind to you."

Louisa met her gaze at last. "He needs your dowry."

Meg's eyes widened. "Surely you don't fault him for that. Most marriages take place to better one or both of the partners."

"You said you wouldn't wed Keane," she retorted accusingly.

"But do I have the strength to resist Grandmama's will?" Meg returned sadly.

"No one should be able to make others wretched because of what they want."

"But Grandmama doesn't think to make us miserable. She really believes she's doing what's best."

"I know." Louisa plucked aimlessly at the coverlet. "But it doesn't prevent the pain."

"You must accept what will be."

"I can't." She sprang from the bed. "Nothing will ever change if everyone accepts things as they are. Can't you see that, Meg?"

"Yes." Lady Margaret looked sadly at her cousin. "But I know I'm not the one to alter the course set for me."

"Then I must. Even if I have to tell him that I know of his treachery."

"Flirting with Lady Badden can't be termed treacherous. We aren't yet betrothed," Lady Margaret tried to calm her.

"He's done more than—" The words congealed in Louisa's throat. If she were to fail, if Meg were to wed Lord Hargrove it would be far better that she didn't know the entire truth. She turned away. "I just want to find Francis."

"Could he be in danger?" Lady Margaret whispered.

"I fear so." Louisa began to pace. "If only we could discover where they are keeping him. What was discovered from the servants?"

"I overheard nothing that could be of use. Lord Brice questioned Aunt Edwina since she had remained at the Retreat that morn. She told him the only thing out of the ordinary was—

"Lud, why didn't I think of this before," she said jumping up excitedly. "You're right, Louisa. He can be rescued!"

"What is it?"

"Aunt Edwina said she was in the gardens shortly before our party returned. She saw two men half-carrying a third toward the Retreat."

"Do you think it was Francis?"

"Lord Cearcy cast a jest about Lord Hargrove needing to keep a closer watch on his wine cellar. Everyone laughed and nothing more was made of it," she explained.

Louisa's excitement faded.

"Aunt Edwina said that one man was rather small and dark."

"Moler?"

"Couldn't it be? But who would dare to hide someone right here? Anyone could discover him?" Lady Margaret sighed.

"What better place?" Louisa considered it. "No one has mentioned searching here. Fortunately I have achieved a fair grasp of how the rooms lay on each floor."

"Surely you don't mean to—" Lady Margaret retreated a step. "Can't we tell the duke what we suspect? If we were to speak to him in the presence of Lord Cearcy or Lord Grenby he'd be forced to order a search."

"It'd never do. He could have Francis moved somewhere else before the search began." Louisa shook her head. "No, you and I must do it."

"You—" Meg paled, "and I?"

"We must rescue Francis," she answered matter-of-factly, her mind already elsewhere.

"Yes," Meg answered, firming her resolve.

"It'll be perfectly safe, Meg," Louisa assured her. "We'll wait until the men go searching, then you and I'll escape Grandmama and begin our quest with the third floor."

Lady Margaret hoped Louisa's plans wouldn't lead to scrapes of the disgracing sort. *What if Francis isn't concealed within the Retreat?* She clasped her hands tightly. *What will happen to us if he is?*

Chapter Sixteen

The determined clink of fork and knife against a plate echoed in the silence filling the breakfast room. Lord Brice's growing concern over the events taking shape didn't prevent a wry smile from gracing his lips at Lord Hargrove's unease and Miss Elliott's new hauteur.

"Your Grace. Your Grace," Lord Brice repeated.

Hargrove removed his gaze from Louisa's bent head and looked at him blankly.

"Shall I see that all is in order for the search groups?" The viscount laid his napkin upon the table.

An uncomprehending blink answered him, then a scowl of understanding appeared. "No, all—yes, please do," he returned his gaze to Louisa.

"Excuse me, Miss Elliott," Lord Brice rose and bowed. "Your Grace." He threw an unheeded wink and sauntered out.

Louisa's throat constricted. Resolutions wavered beneath the caress of Lord Hargrove's troubled gaze. She watched him slowly sip his coffee, trying to fathom his intent.

"Louisa—" Keane smiled at the answering flash in her eyes. "Miss Elliott, I owe you some explanations.

Circumstances prevent me from speaking as freely as I'd wish." He leaned forward, reached to take her hand.

"Your behavior speaks quite well," she interrupted coldly, pulling her hand back. "To any not blinded by your *exalted* position."

"I realize you feel justified in your opinion." Lord Hargrove's pride prickled. "I simply ask that you listen."

"To what? To your protestations of love for my cousin?"

"You know I don't love her." Angrily slapping down his napkin, Hargrove rose.

"Then you admit to misusing Meg's trust?" Louisa continued despite the emotion shaking her.

"Misuse? No, I don't." He glared at her. "Who are you to accuse me?" he taunted, guilty anger overriding restraint.

Louisa was instantly on her feet. "Dare you say I—"

"Yes," Keane stalked around the table. "Who but you would dare to force such a delicate creature to accompany you in a coach through the worst sections of London."

"You—you knew we were following you?" she gasped.

"How many fool's errands have you sent young Medlock on?" he came forward unrelentingly, his features cold and harsh.

Louisa's face turned from alabaster white to beet red. "At least I don't do it for gold," she breathed bitterly.

Verbally struck, Keane stiffened. He took hold of her shoulders. "You're the most aggravating wench to have ever graced my life." As he gazed into her troubled eyes, his ire slowly died. "Louisa, please *try* to understand."

"Remove your hands."

"Then understand this," he breathed and slowly lowering his head, his gaze asking permission, he kissed her soundly.

Louisa's legs turned to rubber, her pulse leaped. She trembled when he lifted his head; her response betrayed her.

Keane reluctantly stepped back.

"Good morn," Lady Badden chirped, breezing into the breakfast room. She ignored the confrontation. "A beautiful morn, isn't it, Miss Elliott," she babbled, arching a brow in sympathy at Hargrove.

"It's an excellent day for finding Mr. Medlock," Louisa answered with cold contempt.

"I was just going," Hargrove said grimly. "Please excuse me, Lady Badden," he gave a slight bow before stalking away.

Lady Badden looked questioningly at Louisa.

Louisa's eyes sparkled angrily. She walked purposefully around the table, a threatening gleam casting a warning.

Lady Badden's aloofness fell away. "I have no appetite this morn," she said, taking her skirts and dignity in hand and departing.

The jingle of harness, squeak of leather, and crunch of restless hooves on the gravel before Hargrove Retreat filled Louisa with nervous anticipation. At the foot of the stairs Hargrove spoke with Lady Thea, the Countess Tember at her side.

"Grenby and Cearcy are each leading a group," he said as those gentlemen mounted. "Brice and I shall take another. Our return is unpredictable. Instruct the cook as you will."

"Lady Margaret will be an excellent hostess during your absence," the countess said, stepping in front of Lady Thea.

"I'll watch out for the women," Lord Badden blustered from the side. "Only wish my gout didn't keep me from riding."

"Someone must remain here in the event that Medlock returns," Hargrove assured him. Nodding at Brice, he walked to his mount and lithely stepped into the saddle. He tipped his hat to the ladies and led the men away at a brisk canter. Out of sight of the main house he slowed the pace.

"What is it?" Lord Brice asked. "Lady Edwina's report?"

"That could've been Medlock."

"That would be very daring of them," Brice commented.

"When has Moler not been?"

"But we checked every chamber below ground last eve."

"Wouldn't it be more cunning to put Medlock in, say, the Gold Room?" Hargrove sidled his mount closer to the viscount's. "Did Miss Elliott hear her aunt's story?"

"No, only her cousin and Countess Tember were present."

"That's a small comfort," Hargrove mumbled to himself. "You were right. It was madness to—" He shook his head, a stern scowl covered his worry. "I was to meet Lady Badden this morn."

"You still could," the viscount noted impassively.

"Yes." Hargrove reined his mount in abruptly, his men followed suit. "First we'll see to Medlock." His jaw tightened. "Do you know she actually believes I'm—" His words trailed away and he motioned the senior groom to his side.

"Lady Badden looked a trifle drawn," Countess Tember said after her ladyship's abrupt departure from the salon moments after the women entered it.

Lady Thea inwardly groaned at being trapped with the countess for the day. "I shall also retire. Such a ghastly business. Oversets the nerves."

Louisa put a hand to her brow. "I don't feel well either. Meg, come to my room and read to me? I always find it soothing."

Countess Tember halted both young women. "Edwina'll attend you. It's time Lady Margaret became acquainted with Hargrove's staff. She'll be their mistress soon," she preened, taking Meg's hand.

"No, you needn't come, Aunt Edwina," Louisa blurted nervously. "I know you want to walk about the gardens," she added with a weak smile. "I'll just rest for an hour."

"I'll gladly read to you," she offered solicitously.

Louisa watched Meg disappear with a sinking heart. "Thank you, but I'll be fine."

"They'll find Mr. Medlock," her aunt reassured her.

Forcing a smile, Louisa nodded, then walked slowly away. As she walked toward her chamber she mulled over her plan.

It's best Meg not come with me. If this goes awry it'll be I who— A mental shake drove the specter of her angry grandmother, of Keane's cold, condemning hauteur from her mind. When she was certain no one would come, she slipped out the door.

Achieving the naturalness of a nervous thief, Louisa made her way down the main stairs. *I'd best go through the kitchen,* she thought and dashed for the east wing.

Safely within the chef's inner ward, she leapt behind a large pie cabinet when a pair of scullery maids entered.

"It's a quiet morn with his grace gone." One put her pan of carrots upon a table not far from Louisa.

"There'll be no rest with her ladyship about." The other began cleaning the leeks. "There's them that say the young one'll be our mistress."

"Then it be true his grace be weddin' soon? Oh, Your Grace!" Both fell into deep curtsies.

Peering around the cabinet, Louisa stifled a gasp at sight of Keane and Viscount Brice.

"Continue with your work," Hargrove ordered curtly, never breaking his stride.

Why've they returned? What'll I do now? tumbled frantically through Louisa's mind. The swinging kitchen door beckoned her. Heeding the impulse, Louisa ran after them.

"Who be that?" the startled maids questioned one another, staring after her.

"Hadn't we best tell cook?" the younger asked.

"Best you learn the house ways. Don't see nothing you ain't supposed to," the other returned with experienced wisdom.

Louisa watched, puzzled as the gentlemen she followed to the third floor thrust open one door, disappeared within, and quickly reappeared. *Are they looking for Francis?* she wondered as she strained to see around the corner.

At that moment Lord Brice beckoned Hargrove from one of the guest chambers. Both men went in, closing the door behind them.

With her heart thumping louder than the soft pat of her satin slippers she tiptoed toward the door. Reaching it, she laid her ear to the door.

"One of your guest chambers, just as you said, Keane. You're better at this business than you know." Silence and then, "There you are, my man," ended Lord Brice.

"This is a ghastly jest," Francis sputtered angrily. "I protest most vehemently—umm—mmmm."

What's wrong? Louisa put a hand on the doorknob.

"What are we to do with him?" Lord Brice was asking. "Can't possibly let him return to the Retreat."

"Nor can we leave him here. Moler may kill him."

Francis's muffled protests tugged at Louisa's sympathy. *I can't let them take him, but how can I prevent it?* She clenched her hands. *I must get a weapon of some sort,* she thought and scurried away.

Running down the corridor near her bedchamber, Louisa passed Meg. "Wait for me," she called back, nearly tripping. "I've found him!"

A weapon, she thought frantically reaching her room. The fireplace poker leapt into sight. Grabbing it, she rushed back into the corridor, down to her cousin, and latched onto her hand as she passed. "I've found Francis," she explained, towing Meg after her. "We must rescue him before it's too late."

The words struck all protest from Meg who raised her skirts and followed pell-mell.

Chapter Seventeen

"Where are we going?" Lady Margaret gasped for breath at the top of the third floor stairs.

"They have him in the fifth room to the left," Louisa whispered. "When we get to the door, stay against the wall so they can't see you. If things go awry, go for help," she explained hurriedly. She tiptoed to the door and listened.

"Is Francis all right?" Meg breathed at her side.

Answering with a shake of her head, she took a firm grip on the poker and slowly eased the door open. With the makeshift weapon now clasped in both hands raised to strike she cautiously moved forward. "Oh, lud."

Wrestling her fear down, Meg inched to the doorway. A hesitant glance into the chamber revealed only Louisa. "Where's Francis?" she asked. "Are you certain this is the chamber?"

Louisa leaned dejectedly on the poker. "They've escaped."

"Perhaps they put him under the bed." Meg ran to the large canopied bed, knelt, and raised the coverlet to peer under it.

"It's no use, Meg. They've taken him elsewhere. I've failed again. If only I'd entered at once—"

Meg turned her head toward the door as Louisa spoke. Raising a finger to her lips she whispered, "Someone's coming."

Louisa pulled her up and pushed her toward the windows. With wildly thumping hearts they leapt behind the floor length satin drapes.

Moler's jaw sagged at the sight of the empty room. *"Sacre bleu! Ou est-il?"* Recovering from his surprise, he ran a practiced eye over the chamber and immediately saw the quivering drapes, and a pair of white satin slippers peeking out beneath them. He went forward stealthily; flicked the curtain back revealing a quailing Meg. "You're one of his grace's guests, *n'est-ce pas?*"

"Yes," she gulped, "I was—was—just looking at—"

"Do you always examine the drapes so closely, *mademoiselle?*" A harsh smile played across his lips.

"Grandmama says one can't be too careful about such things." She edged away from the window, hoping to prevent the Frenchmen from discovering Louisa.

"Your Grandmama should've warned you of the dangers of going about unchaperoned, Lady Hamilton," Moler warned.

"But, Mr. Moler—"

"You know my name? But how?"

"I—I must've heard one of the servants mention it," Lady Margaret twittered nervously, edging forward.

"C'est infortune," Moler muttered, following her, his back now to the windows. He casually withdrew a pistol from beneath his jacket. "I must bid you come with me, *mademoiselle.*"

"I couldn't do that, *monsieur.* Grandmama wouldn't approve." She fluttered her hands wildly. "What've you done with Francis?" she demanded with a boldness that surprised her.

"We'll discuss that later," he cut her off with an abrupt wave of his hand. "You must be taken care of first."

"Oh, I can't watch," Meg jumped nervously, her hands covering her face.

"Quel—"

Louisa rushed the few remaining steps forward, swinging the poker with all her might.

A moment later Meg was staring at the crumpled man, a reddening welt across his forehead. "Is he dead?" she asked.

"I—I don't know." Louisa dropped the poker from her shaking hands.

"What are we to do? Where's Francis? Are you certain you heard him? Oh, dear I don't feel a bit well." Meg began to waver.

"Don't faint, Meg," she clutched her arm. "Take a deep breath. Again. Good." Louisa gulped down a healthy swallow.

"He's still breathing." Relief flooded through her. "Fetch the drapery cording. We'll tie him up and decide what to do with him after we learn what Lord Hargrove and Viscount Brice have done with Francis." She knelt beside Moler's still figure and crossed his arms on his chest.

"They were with Francis?" Lady Margaret said with surprise.

"The cord," Louisa demanded curtly.

"Whatever'll become of us?" Meg asked, handing a piece of the cord to her before fumbling a piece around Moler's legs.

"Keep up your courage—like you did when Moler discovered you, and we'll turn up right yet." Louisa tugged a knot tightly in place.

"I can hardly credit that I didn't faint." Meg smiled faintly. "It's a marvel."

"No, it's not. I've always said you had more courage than you thought. It only needed a reason to show itself."

"Do you truly believe that?" A questioning but pleased smile brightened her.

"Yes." Louisa patted the last knot. "There. Moler will await our return," she added, rising.

"Do you think he is comfortable?"

"Meg!" Louisa rolled her eyes then drew her cousin to her feet. "I'd best take this." She picked up the small flintlock pistol. "It fits nicely in my pocket. Now to find Lord Hargrove."

From a doorway on the second floor Lady Badden saw the two young women pause on the landing and speak animatedly before going down to the main floor. She stepped from the door as they disappeared, paused, then ran lightly up the steps.

"Lady Badden, I've been looking for you," Hargrove said, stepping from behind a huge plane tree in the gardens.

Surprise swallowed, a petulant smile pursed her lips.

"You can't be angry with me," he protested. "I slipped away from the search as soon as I dared," Hargrove murmured.

"They departed two hours ago," she returned coldly.

"I didn't want to raise Brice's suspicions." He cupped her chin and brushed her lips. "You know I couldn't meet you after Medlock's disappearance," he coaxed her.

Lady Badden unbent slightly, brushing his cheek with a kiss. "Of course not. Quite bothersome for you."

"But I'm here now. Walk with me to the maze. No one will interrupt us there." Hargrove drew her arm through his. "I'm desperate for a few moments with you."

"Desperate for me or for the information I've promised?" she teased coquettishly.

Hargrove halted, his hand tightening on her arm. "Do you toy with me?"

"Or you with me?" Lady Badden said icily, her glance cold.

"What ploy is this?" he asked, perplexed.

"You'd not be the first to promise much and give little."

"How can you believe that? What is it? You think I care for the Hamilton chit?" Hargrove laughed, attempted to draw her into his arms.

Lady Badden watched him closely. "Miss Elliott."

Hargrove gave a sharp hoot of laughter, hoping his surprise was concealed. He roughly pulled her to him. "Do you believe I prefer a green stumbling miss to you?" He released her abruptly. "I'll not beg—"

"You're too quick to take offense," Lady Badden told him. "Can't I be jealous?" she purred softly.

"Then you'll help me?" he asked eagerly.

"I'm still trying to learn if much can be gained from the 'work' I mentioned. Gossip can be so unreliable, my dear."

"But time is very scarce."

"Patience, Keane," Lady Badden brushed his cheek with her hand. "Perhaps the morrow's post shall bring the news I await."

"You said you could tell me this morn," he pressed for some commitment.

"I couldn't foresee the difficulty my husband would present. This morn he suggested we leave. Don't look so stricken, Your Grace," she smiled. "You've but to return to London to see me."

"Not if I must flee to the continent to escape the duns."

"Don't worry. Now I insist you return to your men before you're missed. We mustn't encourage the belief that you're responsible for Mr. Medlock's disappearance. Miss Elliott already believes so and isn't reticent about it."

Hargrove bowed. "As you wish, my lady."

As he left, Lady Badden's brow creased. A frown hovered on her lips. "Perhaps I err. But he can be placated if I have."

"Do you suppose they'll return soon?" Lady Edwina asked, looking up from her handwork. "It's been over four hours."

"Must you ask the same question every few minutes?" The countess rose angrily. "Take another walk in the gardens. How vexing of young Medlock to get himself lost."

"Such a discourtesy is upsetting," Lady Thea's look belied her soft tone.

Talbot halted in the doorway of the salon, then approached the marchioness. "The gentlemen are returning, my lady."

"Have they been successful?" she asked, rising.

"I believe so, my lady."

"Go inform Miss Elliott at once," she instructed. "Then see that Mr. Medlock's room is readied with every comfort."

"Yes, my lady," the butler bowed and withdrew.

Lady Thea paused in the doorway. "Shall you come, countess?"

"The gentlemen will surely wish to refresh themselves before seeing anyone," Countess Tember said frostily.

Lady Edwina lifted a brow to the marchioness who nodded her understanding.

"Until supper then," the marchioness answered and left with a smile of satisfaction lightening her features. The clatter of feet on the stairs warned of Louisa's approach near the entryway.

"Is it true? Have they found Francis?" she demanded.

"Is he unharmed?" Lady Margaret arrived at the foot of the stairs, equally breathless.

"We'll learn the answers at once," the marchioness smiled. "They've arrived," she nodded to the large doors through which sounded the clatter of hooves and welcoming shouts. "Calmly, ladies," Lady Thea cautioned as both young women bolted for the doors.

The afternoon sun momentarily blinded them but Francis was readily recognized despite a white bandage swathing his head.

"Francis," Meg murmured and fell into a dead faint.

Only Lord Brice's firm grip kept Medlock from leaping from his mount to aid her.

Hargrove also tossed the young man a warning glance before alighting and hurrying up the steps. "Is Lady Margaret all right?" he asked, going down on one knee beside Louisa who was cradling her head.

Pushing away the vial of smelling salts proffered by the marchioness, Meg spluttered, "Take it away." She blushed deeply at the sight of the crowd gathered about her. "Please let me up."

"Step back," Lady Thea commanded, motioning for Hargrove to help the young lady.

"Fran—Mr. Medlock, you are unharmed?" Meg asked as soon as she was on her feet. "The bandage—"

"A gash, my lady." Lord Brice took hold of Medlock's arm as if steadying him. "It isn't too serious—physically."

Louisa tried to catch Francis's eye. "What do you mean?"

"There is a slight problem with Mr. Medlock's memory," Hargrove answered. "He recalls nothing but riding out yesterday."

"Is that true Francis?" Louisa laid a hand on his arm.

"My head hurts abominably," he muttered, refusing to meet her gaze.

"You'd best take Mr. Medlock to his room," Lady Thea said and took hold of Louisa's arm.

"I've sent for the surgeon," Hargrove told her. "Loss of memory from a severe blow isn't unusual," he looked at Louisa reassuringly. "There's no need to be alarmed."

Lady Badden posed dramatically in the doorway. "It is true then, you're returned, Mr. Medlock."

"But with no memory of what happened," Lord Cearcy chimed as he mounted the steps.

"Is that true, sir?" Lady Badden asked.

Francis put a hand to his bandaged head. "Quite so, I fear."

"Please excuse us, my lady," Lord Brice drew Medlock forward. "Must get him to his chamber."

"Of course," she smiled, stepping out of the way. "You must be dreadfully relieved, Miss Elliott," she simpered.

"I shall be—when his memory returns." Louisa looked pointedly at Hargrove. Giving a low curtsy she raised her chin challengingly.

"Shall we wait until after we dine to have you impart the particulars of the rescue? That is, after all, the proper hour for 'tales.'"

Chapter Eighteen

Lady Badden paused the downward stroke of her hairbrush when she saw a reflection in her mirror. "What are you doing in my chamber?"

Moler decided not to tell her he had just freed himself. "They say Medlock is found." The Frenchman sidled forward. "We must complete the exchange at once, *madame*."

"I don't yet have all the papers." Lady Badden slammed her brush down. "Medlock has no memory of what happened to him or who was involved. He's no danger."

"But the young ladies who—"

"It's Miss Elliott we must take care of. Lady Margaret is too much of a mouse to venture forth alone. Louisa has become bothersome."

"She can't know what—"

"Of course not, but her sort always blunder into the midst of what they shouldn't."

"What papers do you lack? I can't release payment without them," Moler said nervously.

"You'll have the documents. Leave me," she commanded angrily, "and don't show yourself again."

Louisa slammed shut the door of the small salon. "They still won't allow me to see him."

"You mustn't do that," Lady Edwina implored from her chair. "The countess—"

"Oh, Aunt, don't you ever tire of worrying about what Grandmama will think?" Louisa plopped onto the sofa. "Where is she? Still plaguing Meg?"

"You must be more respectful," her aunt reproved her. "And I fear you're right. Lady Margaret is probably being given a medicinal draught."

" 'You must. You must not. You must,' " Louisa mimicked. "It's so tiresome. Oh, never mind," she popped up as quickly. "I'm a nuisance." She kissed her aunt and knelt before her. "Do you ever think of Captain Morris?"

Lady Edwina missed a stitch. "Captain Morris?"

"The gentleman who used to call on you," Louisa prompted.

"That was many years ago." Lady Edwina unraveled a stitch. "What made you think of him?"

"Do you ever wonder what happened to him?"

"I hadn't until the last few days. Lord Cearcy reminds me of the captain." A soft blush stole over her.

"Did the captain wish to marry you?"

"Truly, Louisa, this subject is most indelicate." She made to rise but was stayed by her niece's hands.

"Please, Aunt," Louisa's troubled spirit showed in her face.

"I—I believe he did."

"Then why—"

"Matters were handled differently when I was young," she said, fumbling with her thread. "He'd have spoken to the countess before approaching me."

"And Grandmama wouldn't give him permission to speak. Isn't that what happened?"

"It's the past, child, and best left be."

"But aunt, if someone wished to marry you now, and you cared for him, would you go against her wishes?" Louisa persisted.

"I can't see what that has to—"

"Isn't it the same as Meg refusing to wed the duke?"

"The countess has been determined on the marriage for some time," Lady Edwina answered cautiously.

"He doesn't love her." Louisa rose and swung away. "And Meg isn't strong enough to refuse. If only we had more time."

"Louisa, you're not making sense."

"The only way to save her is to ruin him. But I can't do that. Oh, it's all so confusing." She turned back to her aunt.

"Wouldn't he listen to reason?" Lady Edwina answered timidly. She walked to her niece. "Surely he wouldn't force Meg against her will."

"I wish I could be certain of that," she shook her head.

"Then why don't you give him the opportunity?"

Louisa stared at her aunt for a long moment. "Oh, Aunt Edwina," she hugged her tightly. "What would I do without you?" Tears brimmed in her eyes. "I'll do it at once. Thank you," she kissed her and ran from the salon.

"Oh, dear, what have I done?" Lady Edwina placed her hand to her cheek and stared out of the salon's windows. "Mother will never forgive me if—"

"My dear Lady Edwina," Lord Cearcy's voice boomed behind her. "I had hoped to find you alone. My pardon, my lady, I didn't mean to startle you." He hurried forward.

"My, but you look faint." Cearcy led her to the sofa and sat with her, keeping her hand in his. "Shall I call someone?"

"Oh, no. I was just—rather startled." An attractive blush colored her. "I was thinking of some advice I gave my niece."

"And excellent it was, I am certain," Lord Cearcy smiled, reluctantly releasing her hand. "She cannot err with so good a guide as you, my lady."

Lady Edwina's heart beat as it had not for many years and in a far different manner than when confronted with her mother's ire. "Louisa—Miss Elliott, is an extraordinary young woman. At times I feel rather unsuited for my part in her life."

"You're an extraordinary woman, Lady Edwina, and have prepared your nieces well. Don't fret over Miss Elliott. Come for a stroll with me. The duke has received an excellent example of the *Gouletheria shallon* which was brought from America."

"Talbot, I wish to speak with his grace." A tremor ran through Louisa despite her resolve.

"If you'll wait, miss, I'll see if Lord Hargrove is free," the butler put on his most aloof manner. Finding him in his study he announced, "Miss Elliott wishes to speak with you, Your Grace. She is unchaperoned."

"Bring her at once," Hargrove said without looking up from the papers spread across his desk. When the butler left he rose and strode to the window. The branch before him tugged at the memory of Louisa in his arms—in his heart.

"Miss Elliott," Talbot announced with cold disapproval.

"You may go. Close the door," the duke said without turning. He faced Louisa only after the door clicked shut. "What is it you wish, Miss Elliott?" he asked, his emotions tightly held.

"I don't believe—that you care for Meg—Lady Margaret," Louisa began haltingly, words melting away beneath his stern gaze. "And I've come to tell you that she doesn't care for you—doesn't wish to wed you. In fact, she'll refuse."

"Shouldn't your cousin be telling me this?"

"Meg is—is a delicate creature as you have noted. She's unaccustomed to injuring anyone's feelings, even when her own must suffer. Quite unlike yourself, she doesn't possess the conceit to obtain her desires," Louisa blurted.

"Conceit?" Keane's calm crumbled.

"Isn't it your coronet which impedes you from seeing the views of those less fortunate?"

"And what's the cause of your blindness, Miss Elliott?"

"You've no concept of what life is like for those about you. Accustomed to their bowing and kowtowing at your every whim, you are constantly assured of your inflated self-worth," Louisa said, warming to the subject. "How can you understand Meg's reluctance, nay, horror, at wedding you— or of voicing any objection to the scheme."

"How dare you speak to me in such—"

"Isn't that the whole of the matter, *Your Grace*? Who may dare to cross your wishes? Lord Hargrove's whim is law, isn't it?" Louisa trembled at the anger that burst across his features.

"Law. My word law?" he towered over her. "What do you know of me? What've you seen of my life to justify such a gross exaggeration?" Keane demanded bitterly.

"Yes, I've power but I also have responsibilities. Have you thought of the number of people who depend upon me for their livelihoods? Or how many dullards I'm forced to listen to, how many boorish snobs I must receive courteously, or the politicians endured only because I'm Hargrove?" The duke stared down at her.

"Do you know how it is to never be truly alone? To always have someone only a breath away? To never be able to forget for a moment *who* you are? To realize all seek you out because of your title and wealth and nothing more?"

The anguish in his eyes smote Louisa's heart a wrenching blow. The calm detached voice impaled it.

"Can't you understand, Louisa?" He reached for her, no longer concealing his yearning.

"No—no," she repeated breathlessly, backing away. She bumped into his desk and saw the documents. She pointed a shaking finger. "Those are government papers, aren't they?"

"I'll explain. Give me time," he said, reaching for her.

"But . . ." Louisa weakened, the desire to believe him surged stronger than her fears. She stepped closer, laid a hand on his chest and raised her face to his.

"Mr. Green to see you, Your Grace. He says it's most urgent," Talbot announced at the study's door.

"No," she breathed, "*No.*" She shook free and fled. Tears pressed hotly as Louisa ran headlong down the corridor, away from Hargrove's importuning call. In her room she attempted to gather her thoughts amidst Keane's barrage of counter charges.

How can he be a traitor? How? Is it to protect all those who depend upon him?

An affirmative reply resounded in her. Relief and joy surged. *Then he must be saved for his own sake*, followed close on it. *I can't let him do it. He'd always regret it.* She wiped the tears from her eyes.

Francis'll be able to help me, she thought and hurried to his room.

Upon her entry, Francis edged lower beneath the covers, his fear scarcely concealed.

"Have you recalled anything?" she asked, taking the chair the footman offered.

Francis mutely shook his head.

"Thank goodness you're finally alone," Louisa said, edging her chair closer to the bed. A furtive glance assured her the footman was leaving. "You must help me save Lord Hargrove."

"Whatever do you mean?" Francis looked at her uncomprehendingly. "His grace is bloody well safe in his home."

"But Moler. You can't mean to let him escape. We've bound and gagged him in a guest room on the third floor."

"What's this?" Francis squirmed uneasily. "I don't know Moler."

"You can't have forgotten everything?" Louisa's eyes widened in sudden fear.

Medlock looked away guiltily.

"You don't mean to help me?"

"I implore you, Louisa, for all our sakes, let the matter lie. It's for the best," he begged.

"I hadn't thought you a coward," Louisa rose. "Won't you consider—"

"I can't."

Rising abruptly, she left.

"Lud," Francis said, bringing his fist down angrily on the coverlet. "What'd she mean about Moler?" Throwing back the covers, he rose.

Whatever will I do? Louisa pondered, wandering aimlessly through the corridor. A figure moving stealthily from a chamber far down the hall caught her eye. *Mr. Green.* She sank back against a door. *He has a valise. The documents?* she thought, and moved to follow him.

"There you are," Countess Tember called. "Where have you been? Never mind. Go to your chamber at once and help with the packing. I'll send Lady Margaret's abigail to help."

"But Grandmama," Louisa protested.

"You're to be removed to Hamilton Manor," the countess informed her. "When Medlock is recovered you'll be wed. Go on, child. To your chamber." She stood watching.

"Yes, Grandmama," Louisa reluctantly moved in the opposite direction that Green had taken.

"The coach comes in an hour," the countess told her.

"Yes, Grandmama," Louisa answered with deceiving meekness and hurried away. *Just this once*, she prayed, *let the Fates be with me. An hour. Only an hour. Let it be long enough.*

Chapter Nineteen

Turning the corner to go back to her bedchamber under her grandmother's watchful eyes, Louisa scurried past it and slid to a halt before the door to the servants' stairs. A backward glance confirmed that Countess Tember hadn't followed and she quietly entered. Voices revealed someone on the landing below.

"I'm sorry, my lady, I can't do that," a man's voice floated upward. "Please excuse me, I must see to his grace's instructions."

"But it's what you've done many times," Lady Badden protested.

Creeping down a few stairs, Louisa cautiously peered over the railing. *Mr. Green.* She stifled a gasp.

"Your husband has indicated he wishes all documents handed directly to him from now on. You must speak with him," Mr. Green told her and opened the door on the main floor.

"You must've misunderstood my husband," Lady Badden cajoled. "He depends upon me—"

He speaks of some instructions of Lord Hargrove's,

152

Louisa thought when the closing door cut off the conversation. *Has he already handed over the documents? I'll search his study.*

Easing back into the second floor corridor Louisa prayed her grandmother was gone. "Here at last," she murmured several tense moments later as she approached the study's door. Her hand trembled as she turned the knob. A deep sigh of relief escaped at finding Hargrove gone. Her spirit sank at the sight of the now cleared desktop. "It was too much to hope," she told herself, pausing beside the desk.

She glanced about the room. A leather valise sat beside the desk. Rifling through it, her disappointment increased. "These must be agents' reports," she noted, stuffing the accounting sheets back. Her eyes lit on the three desk drawers.

Wetting her lips nervously, Louisa went through the first and found business papers. Seeing the lock upon the center drawer, her hopes rose. The third drawer held a small derringer which after a brief debate, she slipped into her gown's inner pocket. Then she enthusiastically applied the letter opener from the desktop to the lock of the remaining drawer but to no avail.

"I've the key," Lord Hargrove said, startling her.

Louisa dropped the letter opener.

He walked forward slowly. "You've only to tell me what you seek and I'll give it to you."

"Do you mean that?" Louisa asked, trying to fathom the curious gleam in his eyes.

"On my honor—as a duke." A smile flickered briefly.

"Then don't give the documents to anyone," she pleaded. "Return them to the War Office." Hope soared at his startled look. "I know about Mr. Green. Can't you see how easily you can be found out?" Her words faltered as he gathered her in his arms.

"Think of the dishonor you'll bring on your family, on

yourself." She fought valiantly against the surging feelings his touch, his nearness evoked.

"You've despised my dukedom, even me, from the first time we met. Why do you now wish to save my honor?" Keane asked, drawing her closer.

Louisa misread his smile as mockery and looked down.

"Why do you look away?" Keane caught her chin. "Open your eyes, Louisa," he commanded. "Do you think I mean to laugh at you? Never." He captured her lips, a gentle pledge growing into a demanding thirst.

Warmth spiraled through her, bursting in her mind in brilliant hues as she answered the movement of his lips, pressed closer to him. She sighed in dazed wonder when his lips left hers and brushed softly across her neck as he whispered her name.

"When I've finished the task set for me, I'll explain everything," Keane told her.

"You can't mean to do it," she protested, her heart plummeting. "Tell me you won't." Tears welled in her eyes.

He kissed her tenderly. "You must trust me. I have to finish what I set out upon." Gazing at her lovingly he ended, "No one will ever know if all goes well."

"But I shall."

"Do you love me?"

"Ye—yes."

"Then do as I ask and believe I'm doing nothing that'll bring onus to me or mine." Keane gently cradled her face in his hands and kissed her, carefully reining his desire. "And as much as I regret it, you must go. Countess Tember will be looking for you and it's best you not be found here. Your grandmother will be upset enough by us later." He kissed her again, more lingeringly.

"I'll speak with her as soon as this is over. Now, don't

fret," he led her to the door. Opening it he stole yet another kiss then stepped back reluctantly. "Soon, my love." He assured her, gently nudging her into the corridor. The door closed before she could again plead with him.

Louisa's hand went to the door, hesitated and slowly withdrew it. He'd asked for trust; had promised no harm was to come. *Can't I give it?* she asked herself.

Moler, burst into her mind. *I must talk to Keane about him.* Then. *No, it's best I don't.* She raised a hand to her lips remembering the movement of his. *If he can't find the Frenchman, he can't give him anything.*

But what if he goes looking for Moler? What if the man has regained consciousness? Was the gag tight enough? she wondered, and hurried up the servants' stairs.

Moving from her hastily taken hiding place across the corridor to the left of Hargrove's study, Lady Badden glared at the retreating figure. "So, I was right after all, Your Grace." Her eyes glittered with cold anger. "It was all lies, ploys to use me.

"But it's I who shall set the final scene and you—you'll not only be publicly humiliated as a traitor but also your dear Miss Elliott." She laughed lowly, a newly formed plot filling her thoughts. "I'll enjoy it immensely." Her sharp nails clicked against her ivory fan. "Vastly," Lady Badden laughed softly and went after Louisa.

Who freed him? Louisa pondered, fingering the drapery cord they'd used to bind Moler. *Does he have an accomplice here in the Retreat?* At the sound of the chamber's door opening she whirled about. "Lady Badden!"

"Were you expecting someone else, Miss Elliott? Mr. Medlock perhaps? Tisk, tisk, how will the countess view such doings?"

Louisa moved to pass her. "Excuse me, my lady."

Lady Badden took hold of her arm. "I've a note for you from Lady Margaret."

"From Meg? I don't believe you."

"Just let me give it to you," she said, releasing her hold and reaching into her reticule. She withdrew a small Italian flintlock pistol. Pointing it steadily at Louisa, she smiled. "Let's take a stroll. Moler will be delighted to see you."

"You—"

"Quite right, my dear. Don't try to run away or attract anyone's attention." She motioned with the pistol. "To the servants' stairs." She prodded Louisa with the pistol. "Go down to the main floor," she commanded taking hold of her arm.

Louisa silently cursed Lady Badden's hold, for it was on that side that the derringer was hidden.

On the main floor landing, Lady Badden thrust Louisa toward the exit that lead to the rooms and offices of Hargrove's business agents. A young maid came from one of the rooms as they entered the corridor. She sank into a brief curtsy. "My lady."

"We're here to see Mr. Phillips," Lady Badden told her.

"The door to the left, my lady," the maid answered. She puzzled at Miss Elliott's odd blinking. "Yes, miss?"

"Just a nervous tick," Lady Badden emphatically nudged Louisa with the pistol. "Go about your duties," she dismissed the girl and prodded her captive forward.

"Open the door," she commanded when they reached the third one and then roughly pushed her inside.

Moler sprang up from his chair behind the desk he'd been rummaging through. "Why do you bring this one?"

Lady Badden ignored his question. "Have you found them?"

"*Non.* The documents aren't here."

"Then Hargrove must have them."

"What do you mean to do with *cette mademoiselle?*" Moler asked nervously, his hand going to the angry welt on his forehead.

"For now she'll be our assurance Hargrove'll do exactly as he promised. Where can we hide her?"

"There's a granary at the far end of the gardens. It's shielded by a stand of pines. We could put her there until darkness falls and then have Michel move her," he offered.

"I'll take her. Find something to tie and gag her and meet me there," Lady Badden commanded. She motioned with her pistol to the door. "My dear."

"There you are, Louisa," Francis hailed her as she stepped from the chamber. "The maid said she'd seen you with Lady Badden."

"You shouldn't be out of bed," Louisa told him, casting her head warningly as she stepped back.

"I decided it wasn't safe to let you roam about with the ideas you have," he answered.

"How astute you are, Mr. Medlock," Lady Badden pushed Louisa forward, her pistol now trained on both.

"What?" he gasped in disbelief.

"Do nothing foolhardy, sir. Miss Elliott shall be the first to die." Lady Badden's light tone was belied by the cold glint in her eye, the steadiness of her hand. "Be the gentleman and take her arm. Now isn't that lovely, Moler. The two young lovers shall take a stroll in the garden.

"Go forward but slowly," she commanded. "Moler, I suggest you make all speed. I've an appointment with the duke and he mustn't be kept waiting."

Chapter Twenty

"The coach has arrived. I sent word to Louisa. Now we may wax calm and secure." Countess Tember smiled benevolently at her daughter. She nodded at Lady Margaret. "Perhaps this eve we may celebrate your betrothal."

The young lady looked away. "Can't I go to Louisa?"

"You may bid her farewell when she comes down," the countess answered coldly. "Remove yourself from before that window. Fresh air should never be taken in quantity."

"Yes, Grandmama," Lady Margaret sighed resignedly.

Fifteen minutes crawled by while Countess Tember explained the proper reaction to a proposal from Hargrove.

"How kind of you to come to bid farewell to Louisa," the countess greeted Lady Thea's sudden entry into the small parlor. "She should be here—"

"I fear not, my lady," the marchioness cut her off. "Miss Elliott isn't in her room. The abigail said she never returned to it."

"You must be mistaken." Countess Tember rose, her chin jutting angrily. "Louisa wouldn't dare disobey me."

"If she hasn't chosen to absent herself from the Retreat, I

fear some harm has over taken her," Lady Thea said, looking to Lady Margaret. "Do you know where she may have
gone?" she asked gently.

"She made no mention of leaving. I've been with
Grandmama or Aunt Edwina ever since she was told she
must go to Hamilton Manor."

The countess frowned. "The Retreat must be searched.
When that young miss is found it'll be her last scrape," she
said, with a sharp tap of her fan against the chair's arm.

Lord Hargrove strode into the parlor, anxiety and disbelief
ill-concealed. "Thea, is it true Miss Elliott can't be found?"

"The house is being searched," she answered. "She may
just have gone for a walk," Thea offered weakly.

Keane rounded on the countess. "Why was she leaving?"

"I informed Louisa that she would go to Hamilton Manor
this afternoon. Her behavior isn't suited to so great a house,"
Countess Tember said defensively. "Bringing her with us
was a mistake."

Biting back the acid reproach straining at his lips, Keane
turned to Lady Margaret. "Did you speak with her?"

"Not since Mr. Medlock's return," Meg answered. "Do
you believe something has happened to her?"

"Pardon my intrusion, Your Grace. Ladies," Lord Brice
strode in, a young serving maid in tow. "We have a double
mystery." Turning to the cowering maid he softened his tone.
"Repeat what you told me."

"I—I was jest straighten' Mr. Talbot's quarters jest as
Mrs. Collins told me," she said, wringing her hands. "When
I came out o' the room, there in the hall be one of the lady-
ships and thet young miss who smiles at er'ryone. But she'd
this strange tick. Her ladyship said it were nerves but—"

"Go to the rest," Brice prompted.

"Yes, me lord." She hurriedly dipped into a curtsy. "Her
ladyship asked 'bout Mr. Phillips room and told me to go."

"What of it?" Keane asked impatiently.

The viscount nodded for her to continue.

"In the center hall I was stopped by the young gentleman, the one thet were lost and ye'd fetched back."

"Medlock."

"Mr. Medlock asked if I'd seen Miss Elliott so I told him about the young lady with her ladyship and he went after them."

"Well done," Lord Brice told the girl. "You may go." He shook his head at Keane's unvoiced objection.

"She didn't see them again. In fact, no one has. I checked Medlock's room. Nothing is missing but he."

"Why would Medlock have gone looking for her?" Keane puzzled.

"Pardon me, Your Grace, but it's perfectly clear," the countess said, rising. "And just like Louisa. Never given to propriety, that girl. I'm ashamed to say it, but they've eloped," she announced.

"With Lady Badden as chaperone?" the marchioness asked archly.

"Louisa'd never have eloped. Not with Fran—Mr. Medlock," Meg objected, greatly concerned. "Something dreadful has happened. I know she meant to visit Mr. Medlock to see if his memory had returned. Perhaps it had and they—" her words trailed into guilty silence.

Keane drew aside the viscount. "What part did Lady Badden play in this?"

Lady Badden fluttered into the parlor. "How delightful to find you all gathered together," she simpered. "I've the most enchanting announcement." She nodded at the countess with snide contriteness. "Please do not find fault with my part, my lady."

"Does it concern my granddaughter?"

"And young Mr. Medlock," Lady Badden fluttered her

ivory fan. "They're such a delightful pair, so well-matched, don't you agree? I couldn't resist their pleas. I helped them elope."

Keane squirmed nervously beneath his haughty exterior. Though sure she wasn't telling the truth, he dared not question her. "You'e satisfied, my lady?" he asked the countess.

"Of course it must be true. Dismiss my coach at once," she ordered. "Such a frightfully disappointing child. Come, Lady Margaret," she ordered and stalked from the parlor.

Meg remained where she was, searching for a way to object.

"Come," Countess Tember ordered from the parlor door.

Throwing the duke a desperate plea, she followed in despairing obedience.

Lady Thea started to speak but was silenced by Lord Brice's firm grip on her hand and the warning shake of his head. "Come, Lady Edwina," she said instead. "Won't you walk with us, my lord?" She looked to the viscount.

"Who could resist the company of two charming women?" he smiled, offered an arm to each and escorted them away.

"We're alone, Your Grace," Lady Badden moved forward seductively. "How kind they were to have left us."

"I'm curious, my love," Hargrove said tentatively, "how did you come to help the young lovers?"

"Miss Elliott was a nuisance. I'm happily rid of her. Now my flounces are secure," she returned teasingly. "My present interest is vastly different." She raised her head for a kiss.

"You were not so willing when last we met," Hargrove parried.

"It was jealousy's green head. You can't mean to punish me for it?" she pouted.

Concealing his disgust, Hargrove appraised her.

"No kiss, my love?" she purred, her hands about his neck.
Hargrove brushed her lips lightly, clamping down his
desire to close his hands about her neck.

"That's better, Your Grace." She smiled coldly. "Now we
must attend to business. Tell me, has Lord Devonshire
entrusted you with documents concerning the navy?

"Don't look so angry, my love. My husband is old and a
bore, but he has some advantages," she laughed. "He brings
home such interesting news—and reading material." Her
mood hardened. "Did you bring the navy papers with you
from London?"

"Yes."

"And more have arrived?"

"Need you ask?" he clipped tightly.

"Moler is willing to pay £30,000 for a complete set of sta-
tistics on the present standing of the navy."

"That'd be traitorous."

"It's survival," Lady Badden returned pointedly.

"How do you know Moler wishes this?" Hargrove stalled.

"That, my love, is for me to know. Shall I tell him that you
are willing?"

"Not all the papers have been copied."

"Surely they can be by morn?"

"Yes," Hargrove grudgingly agreed.

"Don't look so unhappy. Didn't you tell me you would do
anything to save your skin from the duns? How much more
is Miss Elliott worth?"

"She's your prisoner?"

"Don't fret about her."

"What is it you want?"

"When the documents are copied, put them in a valise.
Take them to the maze and put them under the hedge at the
northeast corner. *C'est simple, n'est-ce pas?*" she smiled.

"And the payment?"

"The money has already been placed in a bank. When the papers have been authenticated it'll be turned over to me."

Hargrove was taken aback by the coldness, the malicious glint in her eyes. "And what'll I receive?"

"Why, I thought that was amply clear, Your Grace," Lady Badden smiled. "I must go."

"Not before some assurance."

"You've my word that Miss Elliott shall be—released—if all is done as agreed. I must go," she said and kissed him lightly. "It'd never do to arouse suspicions." Fluttering to the door she turned with a curtsy. "We're agreed?"

"By morn."

"No later than seven."

Hargrove nodded and watched her leave. When she was gone, he smashed a fist into his palm.

"You could injure your hand doing that," Lord Brice attempted a jest as he entered the parlor from a second door.

"Are the grounds being searched?"

"Very carefully—to arouse no suspicion."

"Do you have any hint at what has happened to them?"

"Medlock must have lost his resolve. Miss Elliott can be persuasive," the viscount offered.

"Even if he didn't do as we agreed, it doesn't explain this." He shrugged. "I must find them."

"I don't think they'll harm her until after Moler has the papers."

"You think Lady Badden isn't to be trusted?" He waved aside a reply.

"We simply must close the trap very carefully and much sooner than we planned," Glynn calculated.

"I don't know. Something about Lady Badden is—"

"You grow too skittish, Keane. We've the papers and she wants them badly. Badden hinted he means to divorce her."

"That only makes her more desperate. More dangerous."

"Don't think the worst. She may know about your interest in Miss Elliott, but not about our plans. Medlock may have led Louisa on some wild chase and Lady Badden is capitalizing on it."

"I pray that you're right, my friend. It'd be devilish bad for him if any harm comes to her," he stated with certainty.

Moler moved furtively through the corridors of Hargrove Retreat until he reached the second floor guest chambers. With a light tap at the door, he slipped inside.

He hid in the shadows until he was certain Lady Badden was alone in the great bed. Moler wished again he had never gotten involved with her. "All is well, *madame*," he said.

She sat and lit a candle. "They searched the grounds and outer buildings?"

"The fools thought no one would notice them, but, yes, it was done as you said. They found nothing." Moler grinned. "One of the grooms came to look inside the granary but I hinted that an assignation was taking place and that he'd lose his position should he interrupt it."

"Cleverly done."

"Is all arranged for the morn?"

"The valise shall be in place by seven. Take it to the ship at once."

"Mr. Medlock and the young lady?"

"There's a bottle of laudanum on my dresser. Give them enough to ensure their sleeping till morn and have them placed beneath the false seats in my coach." She tossed a curl off her shoulder. "They'll suffer a dreadful accident."

"It'd be far less risk if I attended to them this eve. The bodies wouldn't be found for many days," Moler grumbled.

"Do only as I've ordered," Lady Badden warned sharply.

"*Oui, madame*." Moler bowed, relieved his features were

in shadow. She was far too dangerous to trust and in this instance too dangerous to obey.

He dared not contemplate what would happen if she discovered the agreement he'd struck with Hargrove. The duke had sent a note telling him their pact would be completed in the morn.

Miss Elliott and Mr. Medlock are also guarantees for me.

Biding farewell, he took the laudanum and slipped away. *I'll not kill them until I have the papers. C'est trop de dangereux.* He congratulated himself. *The papers will soon be in hand and not a sou to anyone. Napoleon'll reward me.*

Chapter Twenty-one

Moler took the carefully wrapped packet of papers from Hargrove. "*Merci monsegnieur.* This is the authority over the account which was placed with Pierce and Son in London as agreed."

"A very tidy process."

"*Mais, oui.*" The Frenchman flashed a smile. "That's why it was acceptable to you, *n'est-ce pas?*" he asked, his own pleasure deepened by the knowledge that the funds were being withdrawn that same day.

"And what does Lady Badden know of our meeting?" Hargrove asked, his eyes flashing up from the parchment in his hand.

"We're men of business." Moler shrugged expressively. "You gratify *madame* by your part and have doubled the figure that she's given. Everyone is pleased."

"Quite right." Hargrove smiled coldly, calculating just how much the man knew.

"So you'll give me the other documents now?" Moler held out his hand.

"No, it'll be best to adhere to the agreed plan, especially

since the payment has altered," Hargrove said, watching him closely.

"Altered? Ah *oui*." Moler rubbed his chin contemplatively.

Hargrove laid the bank draft on his desk. "I don't think Lady Badden would be well pleased if she knew we met this morn, and I'd not be pleased if harm came to the new 'collateral.' "

"Of course. It'll be as you wish," Moler said, irritated by the unvoiced threat. He flashed a smile filled with gloating triumph as he turned away.

His papers shuffled into a neat stack, Hargrove rose and walked to the window. The lawns before him glistened with dew but he saw only the reflection of a laughing face that suddenly turned fear-stricken. With a stern mental shake, he reached for his watch fob, removed the gold timepiece and snapped it open. "Only thirty minutes left. Glynn and his men should be in place." He drew a deep breath, then tugged at the bell cord.

"Yes, Your Grace?" Talbot asked, appearing at once.

"Take word to the Countess Tember that I wish to see her in an hour. I'll await her in the library."

"As you wish." Talbot bowed but hesitated to leave. "Pardon my impertinence, Your Grace, but you appear troubled. May I be of assistance?"

"Doing as I ask will be enough." *If Talbot suspects something, what of Moler? Lady Badden?* he mused uneasily, and went to the window once more.

"Your Grace."

The call brought the duke from his melancholic reverie some time later. "It's time, Your Grace." Mr. Green laid a leather valise on his desk.

Lord Hargrove touched it. "They'll suspect nothing?"

"The first few pages are quite authentic but they reveal little. Lady Badden and Moler are only couriers from what we have learned. Certainly, her ladyship can't judge their value."

"I suppose it doesn't matter if they could," Hargrove returned pensively.

Green smiled. "Not with our plans for them, Your Grace."

"Very well." He took the valise in hand. "All is in place? The men have been instructed?"

"Yes, Your Grace. No one will act without Lord Brice's signal. If Moler leads him to Mr. Medlock and Miss Elliott, we'll have the pair back safely," Green told him as he held the door for Hargrove.

Lord Hargrove poured a glass of sherry and sipped it absentmindedly. The pleasant intermingling odors of beeswax and leather bindings remained unnoticed, as did the wall of books and manuscripts in which he took much pride. *Louisa.* She filled his thoughts. *Is she safe? Why did I allow myself to be shackled here, helplessly watching?*

"God help her," he muttered, lowly, cursing the wisdom that bound him to sit and wait.

"I trust that is not all you'll have to say at this unreasonable hour," the Countess Tember noted with haughty irritation at the library's door. Her features mellowed as she entered. "One must bear with a youngster's impatience."

"My lady, thank you for coming," he said, ignoring the implication. "A glass of sherry? I've heard it said it removes the morning chill from the joints."

"Very well. As a tonic."

"Of course, my lady. Do be seated," Hargrove said handing her the stemmed glass. "I've received information regarding Miss Elliott."

"I've no desire to hear it," she snapped. "That ungrateful child." She clamps her lips together adamantly.

Hargrove sharply reined his temper. "Miss Elliott and Mr. Medlock didn't elope. We fear they've been kidnapped."

"Abducted? What nonsense," hooted the countess.

"Louisa—Miss Elliott learned I was involved with a Frenchman interested in purchasing certain government documents to which my position in Parliament gave me access."

"I told her that the very thought that you would consider doing such a thing was absurdly foolish," she reassured him.

"But it wasn't," he snapped. "It's true and we believe the agent I am dealing with now has Louisa and Medlock."

"Dear God," the countess gasped. "You're a—a traitor? Lud," she was speechless, all her careful planning gone awry.

"I'm only a ploy to trap a traitor, someone far more desperate than you," he answered coldly.

The countess swallowed, realizing the implication of his words. She recovered quickly. "And you had the audacity to endanger Lady Margaret's life?"

"Not a thought for Louisa? She's suffering the consequences of my foolhardy invitation," Hargrove said acidly.

"Why on earth *did* you invite us?" her ladyship asked, her anger stirred to cover a surge of guilt. "Was your promise to wed Lady Margaret but another ploy?" Countess Tember rose.

"I gave my word to wed *one* of your granddaughters and I intend to keep it, God preserving her."

"Louisa!?"

Lady Badden restlessly paced in her bedchamber. Pausing before the full-length glass, she admired the military cut of her traveling gown and the rakish shako-styled bonnet. "I'll be vastly admired," she said as she ran a hand down her hip. "His grace'll pay dearly for daring to pretend with me. He'll not only lose the Retreat but Miss Elliott." A malevolent smiled gazed back at her.

A soft tapping at her door hurried her to it. "What has kept you?" Lady Badden irritably demanded of Moler.

"One mustn't be too precipitate in such matters," he answered. "You must examine the papers as we agreed."

"Then let me see them. I wish to be gone from this place."

Moler opened the valise and dumped the papers on her bed.

Lady Badden scanned the first few pages. "They appear to be what was promised." Drawing several papers from the center and studying them, puzzlement clouded her features.

"It was very wise of you to learn so much from your husband, *madame.* Such a bloody shame, as you English say, that we must part our ways."

"What?" She glanced up, her eyes widening slightly at sight of the pistol in his hand. "*You* think I meant to trick you with these?" Lady Badden said, mistaking the reason for his action. "Then the duke makes fools of us both."

"What do you mean?" He advanced nervously. "What's wrong with the documents?"

"They are the same ones I gave you a score of weeks ago," she said casting them aside.

"*Sacre bleu! Tend-il une trappe?*"

"If it is, he's the one to fall into it," Lady Badden said, realizing how badly she'd been duped. "No one plays me for the fool." She snapped the valise shut. "Go to the stables and secure two mounts."

"But your coach?"

"While I speak to his grace about the error he made, you'll ready the horses and tether them with yours. Then go to the granary and take care of Mr. Medlock. Don't harm the girl."

He nodded his understanding.

"We'll be in France before they discover his body."

"Without the proper documents we'll not be—"

"I believe his grace possesses them. I'll get them."

She drew a dual-barreled derringer from her reticule. "Await me at the granary."

"Oui, madame," Moler bowed and hurried away.

Lady Badden tugged at the bell cord in her chamber and then slowly drew on her gloves. "I wish to speak with Lord Hargrove," she told the maid who came in answer. "Learn where he is."

The young girl returned in a few moments. "His grace is in the library, my lady. Do you wish Mr. Talbot to see if he is free?"

"No, I'll go myself," Lady Badden answered, floating past the maid, her steps unhurried.

Hargrove pressed a glass to Countess Tember's lips. "Drink this,"

She swallowed obediently.

"I realize it must be a shock for you," he said, handing her the glass. "But I love your granddaughter very much."

"Everyone loves Lady Margaret," the countess said stubbornly. "She's the most malleable—"

"You can't have misunderstood me, my lady," Keane's tone hardened. "Your manner speaks ill of your sensibilities. It's Louisa I'll wed."

"May I be the first to offer my felicitations, Your Grace?" Lady Badden stood framed in the library's doors. "I regret I won't be able to attend the wedding, but then, neither shall there be a bride." She entered and closed the doors.

Hargrove glared at her contemptuously.

"Why, Your Grace, you never looked so when you held me in your arms," she purred dangerously.

"Harlot," swore Countess Tember, realization of the danger not quite dawning. "Don't you dare harm Louisa."

"Hold your tongue, old woman, before the temptation to silence it becomes too great."

Seeing the derringer, the countess sank back in alarm.

"What do you hope to gain?" Hargrove asked scornfully.

"I didn't realize the depth of your deception until Moler showed me the documents. You wished nothing less than my betrayal," she accused, her color rising.

"And I have it."

"Silence. Bind and gag the old woman if you don't want her harmed," she commanded. "Now." The pistol moved in the direction of the countess's head. She slowly cocked it.

"Do as she says," the countess snapped. "Don't try to take her, her accomplice may kill Louisa."

"This won't help you," Keane told Lady Badden as he bound the countess's hands.

"No one will stop me as long as I've you, Your Grace," she answered, then inspected the bindings. "Well done. Now let's go find the papers which you were supposed to give Moler."

"If I refuse?"

"Then Miss Elliott dies."

"Should we take them now, yer lordship?" the man beside Lord Brice whispered urgently.

"No," the viscount clipped, watching the doors of the stable the Frenchman had entered a short time before.

"Why's 'e gettin' more horses. One's already at the granary?" the agent questioned when Moler emerged leading two saddled steeds. "Why they be side-saddles," he exclaimed lowly.

"Quiet," Brice hissed. Something had gone awry, for Lady Badden's coach was standing ready in a shelter of pines not far from the Retreat. "Follow me in a few moments," he ordered curtly and crept after Moler.

The Frenchman tethered the horses beside his own outside the granary. After scanning the gardens carefully, he slipped inside.

A gleam of inspiration glittered in the viscount's eyes as he watched from a distance. "Let's see what you're about, *monsieur,*" he muttered, and slunk forward from bush to bush. Reaching the granary, he drew a pistol from his belt and pressed his ear to the door.

Moler stood over his prisoners. "*Mademoiselle et monsieur,* I've come to bid you farewell. Our plans have changed but the end is the same; just a little delayed for you, *mademoiselle.*" He drew a garrote from his pocket and moved toward Medlock.

"It's a much kinder end than her ladyship would have given you." He wound the cord around Francis's neck.

Chapter Twenty-two

"*Arretez*—halt." Lord Brice's deadly voice filled the dusty bin.

Moler slowly straightened. "I was about to free this young man." He moved a hand slowly to his pocket.

Looking up from the floor, Louisa saw the glitter of steel beneath the Frenchman's cape. She threw herself against him just as his hand touched the hidden stiletto's handle. Moler sprawled forward, the blade tumbling harmlessly to the ground.

"Well done," the viscount bowed to Louisa. "Unfasten Miss Elliott's gag," he motioned threateningly with the pistol. When Moler had finished, the viscount handed him a small silver flask. "Give her a sip."

Sputtering, Louisa managed a hoarse, "Lady Badden."

"I know." Lord Brice's features darkened. "I'll take care of her as soon as you're safe. Untie Mr. Medlock, Moler."

The Frenchman raised his hands hopelessly. "The knots, *ce sont trop de deficile.*"

"Step back," Lord Brice ordered as he reached down to pick up the stiletto. "Further," he warned. Going down on

one knee beside Louisa, he slashed the cords binding her
hands and legs. "Rub your legs before you try to stand," he
advised.

"Where is Lord Hargrove," she asked.

"In her ladyship's care," Moler spat venomously.

They all looked at him.

"You think to fool us with the old documents? Bah!" He
snapped his fingers. "That's what the duke's life is now
worth."

Louisa struggled to her feet. "What do you mean?"

"Ask his lordship," Moler bowed contemptuously at the
viscount, his eyes darting to the pistol, to the young lady and
back.

Louisa momentarily stood between his weapon and Moler.
The Frenchman leaped forward, pushing her against Brice.
As they struggled to remain upright, he dashed for freedom
only to be fouled by Francis who rolled against his legs.

Recovering, Moler scrambled for the fallen stiletto and
popped up in front of Lord Brice. A practiced flick of the
blade sent the viscount's pistol thudding to the floor.

Louisa watched the two men warily confront one another.

"Go to warn Keane," the viscount ordered, his eyes never
leaving Moler.

Louisa glanced at Francis and then sprinted from the
granary. She hurtled through the closest door of the east
wing and on through the corridors. Louisa collided with
Talbot as she entered the main hall.

"Miss Elliott!" the butler exclaimed taking in her dusty,
disheveled appearance. "Where have you been? I must
report this to Countess Tember at once."

"Where's Lord Hargrove? I must see him," she gasped,
taking in deep breaths.

"You can't see his grace in your present state," Talbot
protested.

"Tell me where he is."

The butler frowned then said reluctantly, "In the library, miss. With the Countess Tember."

Dashing away, Louisa plummeted into the library, her heart sinking at finding it empty.

"Ummph—umm—ummm," came from the far sofa.

Her heart in her throat, Louisa edged toward it. "Grandmama!" she gasped in relief. "Let me undo this." She fumbled at the gag's note, cursing her still numb fingers.

"Thank God you found me," the countess said as soon as her lips were freed. "That mad woman, Lady Badden has—"

"Where is she, Grandmama? Where's Lord Hargrove?" she demanded taking hold of the countess's shoulders.

"She took him to find some papers. This is a veritable nest of spies," she answered, holding up her bound hands. "Where are you going," she protested. "Don't leave me like this."

Dear God, she thought, *the child will get herself shot*. "Talbot!" the countess screamed.

Lady Badden cautiously leafed through the documents Hargrove had placed on his desk. "These are much better, Your Grace. No, keep your hands on the chair," she raised the derringer even with his heart.

"Will you free Miss Elliott now?"

"When I'm safely away. You must see we're not followed or I won't be able to promise that she'll be spared."

"Did you know that Moler made a separate bargain with me?" he said, trying to delay her. "I see you didn't."

"It makes no difference," she answered, and began placing the documents in the valise. "He's lost his usefulness in any event," Lady Badden snapped angrily. Running steps in the corridor caught her ear. She backed to the door.

Louisa burst into the study. She flashed a huge relieved

smile at finding Keane safe. "Lord Brice sent me to warn you about Lady Badden."

Lady Badden stepped into view. "Too late, my dear."

Louisa lunged as Lady Badden fired the derringer. The ball twanged loudly; Louisa fell back against the door. Leaping from his chair, Keane grabbed hold of Lady Badden, wrestling the pistol from her hand. She released it and gave him a mighty shove. While he strove to catch his balance she dashed from the study.

Hargrove rushed to Louisa. He knelt, turned her over gently. When her eyelids flickered, he breathed, "Thank God," and crushed her to his chest. When she squirmed he held her back, his eyes raking across her for sign of a wound.

Fumbling at her pocket, Louisa rubbed her hip beneath it. "The shot must have hit Moler's pistol," she grimaced. When he had eased her up she saw that Lady Badden was gone.

"Where is she?" Louisa demanded. "Go after her."

"You must go to your room at once," Keane told her as he helped her stand. "Brice'll take care of Lady Badden."

Talbot lurched into the study. "Your Grace, you must come at once—Lady Badden has fallen down the stairs. I fear she's dead."

"Go now," he ordered Louisa. "Do you hear me?"

"Yes." She twisted away and stumbled blindly past the worried butler.

Keane followed her into the corridor. "See that Miss Elliott goes to her room and then fetch her aunt for her," he told Talbot in a tone that demanded instant obedience. "I'll take care of Lady Badden." After the butler had gone, he hurried to the landing and down the stairs. At the bottom Lady Badden lay surrounded by several maids and footmen.

"Fetch a surgeon," Hargrove told a footman. After failing to find a pulse, the duke removed his coat and covered her face. "Fetch something on which to carry Lady Badden to her chamber."

"Keane?" the viscount questioned gazing down at the body.

Hargrove rose. "It's finished."

Lord Hargrove entered the small parlor where his guests, except for Louisa and Lord Badden, had gathered just as the long case clock struck eleven that eve.

Francis Medlock moved forward from the fireplace. "Lord Badden?"

"He'll leave with his wife's body in the morning."

Those in the room nodded solemnly.

Lady Margaret rose. "And Moler?"

"Under escort to London. The government hopes to learn his contacts. His presence here is to be forgotten."

"I think we should all retire," Lady Thea said, moving to her husband's side. She took his arm and they left.

"Yes," agreed Lord Cearcy and escorted Lady Edwina out.

"We'll remove to Hamilton Manor in the morning," the countess announced.

Francis started nervously. He fidgeted with his cravat until his eyes met Lady Margaret's, then he bowed to the countess. "May I speak, my lady?"

"As if I could prevent it," Countess Tember sighed. "If I forbid this match?" She cocked a brow at Lady Margaret.

Meg trembled, then blushed and went to Francis's side. She laid a hand on his arm. "I'll wait until I reach my maturity if I must," she said firmly.

"There's no need." The countess sniffed loudly. She looked away from the happy pair. "We'll set a date on the morrow."

"Oh, Grandmama." Meg ran to her, embraced her and kissed her cheek.

"Go before I change my mind about this foolishness," the old woman said stiffly.

Giving her another kiss, Meg took Francis's hand.

"Only one turn about the garden," Countess Tember called after them.

"A glass of sherry?" Lord Hargrove inquired.

"Yes, my joints are stiff again. The night air," she said, accepting the glass. "You won't recant."

"No," he smiled. "May I have your permission?"

"If I refuse?"

"Do you hate her that much?" he asked softly.

"You don't understand."

"That you are punishing Louisa for her mother's indiscretion?"

A startled expression rose to her features. "That's not true."

"Her mother married without your permission."

"And learned to regret it. A love match. Bah! She died a pauper," Countess Tember said bitterly.

"In disgrace?"

She rounded on him pointing her finger defiantly. "Yes. And Louisa is exactly like her—" The words faded, her hand fell to her side.

"It would please me greatly, for Louisa's sake, if you would give your approval to our marriage should she accept me," he said quietly. "But the lack of it won't prevent it if she does."

There was timid knock on the door. Lady Edwina edged in nervously. "Excuse me, Your Grace, but Louisa is gone from her chamber. I thought I'd check before I retired and—"

"Never fear," Hargrove assured her. "Talbot?" he looked past her to the butler.

"In the gallery, Your Grace."

"You've my permission," Countess Tember said as he made to leave. "Please tell Louisa that I—I ask her forgiveness."

"I'm certain you'll have it." He flashed a smile and strode out.

Lady Edwina wrinkled her brow. "Whatever did he mean? Why, Mother, you're crying."

Countess Tember brushed aside her daughter's hand. "A piece of soot from the fireplace. You'd better retire. Late hours makes a woman of your years unattractive. Tell my abigail she is to curl your hair in the morn." She blew her nose.

"I was thinking that Lord Cearcy might wish to see the gardens at Hamilton. Yes?" she snapped irritably at Lady Edwina's gaping wonderment.

"I—I suppose I could invite him," Lady Edwina swallowed her amazement.

"Then do it," Countess Tember commanded and left the parlor.

Taking the sconce Talbot carried, Keane nodded his dismissal and entered the gallery. The candles flickered in the gloom of the long, narrow chamber.

"Louisa?" Hargrove called gently. He set the sconce on a side table and walked to the figure standing deep in the shadows. He tenderly gazed down at her, her features growing more distinct as his eyes adjusted to the dim light. "Louisa," he repeated softly, reaching out.

"Is she dead?" she asked dully.

"Yes. She would have been destined for the hangman had she lived."

"And everyone's honor is quite safe now," Louisa said, her voice cracking. "Am I to leave on the morrow?"

"Yes, to lay plans for Lady Margaret's wedding."

"I see."

Keane gently lifted her chin. "She and Francis shall deal well together."

"She and—Grandmama has given her permission?" she exclaimed.

He smiled. "Permission for both of her granddaughters' marriages."

"I knew you meant to ridicule me." Louisa burst into tears; struggled to escape his hands.

"Listen to me," Keane gripped her shoulders. "I love you. I have since I first saw you glare so provokingly at me with sawdust and spider webs cloaking you that day in the park."

Louisa raised tear-filled eyes to his. "Please let me go."

"Not until you tell me you don't love me, my dearest scapegrace."

"Why do you mock me?" she whispered into the folds of his cravat, her hands lightly against his chest.

"Does this say I mock you?" He raised her face, his lips closed on hers, demanding a response. "How can you believe I don't love you?" Lord Hargrove kissed her eyes, her throat, and then captured her lips once more.

The choking fear that had filled Louisa since he had told her to go to her room began to dissolve. "But I'm a shameless failure in all of the social graces," she protested weakly. "Grandmama says I'll always be hopeless."

"Your grandmother asked me to tell you she wishes your forgiveness," Keane held her tenderly.

"She—does?"

"She loves you dearly," he said, "as I do. And your scrapes shall be the perfect remedy for my awful pride. Not that you will have time for many." He kissed her lingeringly.

Louisa pulled back several moments later. "But if I ever disgraced you—"

"Never," he promised. "What was a scrape for Miss Elliott

shall be mere fashion for the Duchess of Hargrove. But . . ." he straightened suddenly.

"What?" she asked in alarm.

"Can you forego climbing trees?"

"Keane—"

"It would set a bad example for our children."

"Keane!" A sudden shyness crept over Louisa.

"Glynn was correct once again." His teasing smile grew larger at her puzzlement. "I told him about you after that encounter with the log. He said you'd be very important to me." He gazed at her filled with longing. "Say you love me."

"Can you forgive me for all I thought?"

He cocked his head warningly.

"I love you," Louisa breathed, her eyes glowing with her love. She met his lips willingly, answering his hunger with her own while the Hargroves' ancestors hanging above them gave unspoken approval to the next addition to their number.